T0208698

Lysa

Karin (Caulien) Breuer

WestBow Press books may be ordered through booksellers or by contacting:

WestBow Press
A Division of Thomas Nelson & Zondervan
1663 Liberty Drive
Bloomington, IN 47403
www.westbowpress.com
1 (866) 928-1240

ISBN: 978-1-9736-4933-5 (sc)
ISBN: 978-1-9736-4934-2 (e)

Library of Congress Control Number: 2018914893

Print information available on the last page.

WestBow Press rev. date: 1/15/2019

Dedication

This story is dedicated to all the women who are survivors of abuse. May you continue to know that the hand of the Lord will always guide you to safety.

Thanks

My sincere gratitude goes to Joan Smith, my dear friend, who encourages me to write, reads, edits and critiques my writings unabashedly.

Introduction

The story of Lysa was inspired by a story which my mother told me some twenty years ago about a great aunt. The story kept haunting me because it is such a well-known story re-played in many families by aunts, sisters, daughters, mothers, with varying outcomes.

My mother said that my great-aunt continued to live with her husband after a dramatic evening when she put her life on the line. Her husband binge drank and then would beat her mercilessly. One night, when he had gone out again to drink, she decided she was never going to be beat again. Stopping him at the door with a barrage of flying dishes and utensils, she confronted him. She gave him the option of killing her now or stopping his drinking and never laying a hand on her again in anger. Apparently, he was taken aback by her gutsy confrontation and stopped drinking. He never beat her again.

Lysa is not my great-aunt who lived at the turn of the 20th century. Lysa became a real, living person the longer I wrote her story. In the end, she told me when to stop so that you too might engage with her and find yourself continuing to explore the story in the next chapter of her life

Lysa

Lysa looked at the clock. 8:00 p.m. She knew that he would not be home now until almost midnight. She knew he would be drunk. She knew that this time he could kill her in his drunken rage. This time she was ready. She would not die tonight without a fight.

Lysa cleaned up the kitchen methodically as she had done now for the past four years. She put away the untouched dinner, cleared the carefully set table and washed the counters. She emptied the dishwasher; but here her routine changed. Instead of putting the dishes back into the cupboards she set them carefully on the clean kitchen island that also served as their table positioned kitty-corner from the door that he would come through. Having done that she set to emptying the drawer with the kitchen knives and finally the cupboard that held the china his grandmother had given them on their wedding day, carefully laying everything out in rows on the island. It was 9:00 p.m. when she sat down at the table and faced the door. Today it would be different. Today she would not cower and take the blows while begging him to forgive her for yet one more complaint that he threw at her. She felt her new-found strength coursing through her body and an inner calm that came with that strength.

This morning, after he had gone to work, she had showered and then stood at her dresser deciding how she might color her hair so that he might be more pleased with her appearance. He had called her "dowdy" last night and said she was letting herself go. He was not pleased. She had stood there looking into the mirror at her thick chestnut colored hair, her pale skin and her shockingly empty eyes when she had an epiphany. Staring back at her from the mirror Lysa saw the woman she had once been. Her heart raced. Yes, that same Lysa was still there, behind the lifeless dark brown eyes waiting for the moment that she would recognize herself again. Lysa lived; this re-discovered Lysa, the Lysa that she had once been, would not die without a fight. There would be no cosmetic make-over. Tonight, she would be ready for him.

Lysa breathed in deeply, made herself a cup of tea and deliberately began to remember; to re-live every moment of that wonderful day, the day of her wedding and the culmination of two years of magical courtship. She needed to know how she came to this hour; what had happened in four short years that she should today fear for her life. She needed to remember the whole journey because she could not afford to underestimate her role in what she had allowed herself to become. Her strength, the strength that had filled her all day depended on her not being blind-sighted tonight by either his charm or his abuse.

Lysa recalled the first day Adolf had walked through the door of her modest ladies' apparel shop. He was tall and slim. His hair was dark brown, cut short except for an unruly lock that fell onto his forehead almost covering the brow over his right eye. He had walked directly over to her and addressed her in a cultured baritone voice, "Good afternoon, Miss. I am looking for a pashmina shawl for my grandmother's birthday. Do you carry them?"

She had been aware that something inside her changed in that moment. She paused as she recalled that feeling, giving herself permission to explore what she had felt that day. He had created an inner dissonance; her heart seemed to beat faster and her hands had felt clammy. The uniqueness of the feeling he had created in her both attracted and frightened her. She served him professionally; chose a paisley shawl in the colors that he said his grandmother loved—rich colors of fall: deep orange, brown and gold with a touch of moss green-- and boxed it in a soft yellow colored box that bore the name of her shop "Lysa" printed in a pale peach hue. She tied the box with peach ribbon and completed the sale. He had thanked her and had walked out of the door. Only then did she fill her lungs again with a deep breath and willed her heart rate back to its normal rhythm.

By the time Lysa returned home that evening she had regained her composure. Her mom had dinner ready for them as was her habit. Lysa poured two glasses of red wine and put them on the table before they both sat down for their evening meal. Lysa's mom chatted about her day and as usual asked her daughter how the day at the shop had gone. Lysa told her mom that she had had a quiet day but had made enough sales to satisfy her accountant who had come in for an hour to review the week's books. Something inside her kept Lysa from telling her mother about the encounter with the tall slender stranger.

Following the death of her father three years ago, Lysa had accepted her mother's invitation to move back home. It was a comfortable life for the two women and they had grown close. While her mother did not pry into Lysa's life, she knew her daughter well enough to know that Lysa had omitted part of the day's events.

Lysa's mother was proud of her daughter's accomplishments. Lysa had gone to college to study business after graduating from high school and discovered in her final year that she was drawn to merchandising. After receiving her degree, Lysa had sought out an apprenticeship as a fashion buyer with an upscale boutique, found a small apartment to rent and honed her skills as both a buyer and a salesperson. At the end of her two-year apprenticeship, the company had offered her a position and while Lysa was flattered by the offer, she was beginning to envision herself as an entrepreneur. The two years in the city had given her a vision of a niche market that she felt she could fill, using her skills to bring style to the middle-class career women with whom she related.

While she was still debating how she might accomplish her goal, her father had a fatal heart attack. Lysa inherited a modest sum of money and when her mother suggested that she move back home, Lysa decided to accept her mom's offer and to use her inheritance to open a business of her own.

In the six months following her father's death, Lysa created a business plan, found an affordable location for her shop in a neighbourhood dotted with other small shops and restaurants within walking distance of a cluster of office buildings, a medical clinic, a fitness gym and a high school. It was perfect for the clientele Lysa wished to attract. While she knew that she would never become rich in this business, the past two and half years that the store had been open had provided her with a better than modest living. She was able to hire a shop assistant and an accountant and already had a well-established clientele that appreciated her taste in fashion as well as her ability to locate special items that her regular customers occasionally asked her to find.

College, apprenticeship and a new business had consumed much of Lysa's time. Although she had friends and occasionally dated, she had neither the time nor the desire to make time for a genuine relationship. On the occasion that her mom would start asking questions about her lack of social life, Lysa would laugh good-naturedly and say "I'm not even 29 yet mom. I'll start to worry after my thirtieth birthday. I promise I won't give 'Mr. Right' the brush-off when he waltzes through my door." And, while the two women cleared their dinner dishes and put away the left-overs, Lysa mused about "Mr. Right". Had he stepped through her door today?

It was six weeks, almost to the day when the stranger walked through the door of her store once more. He wore a light blue sport shirt that was open at the collar under a silver grey cardigan, dark grey slacks and soft grey leather shoes. His mouth was open in a wide smile that showed even white teeth as he approached her. He spoke as he handed her a bouquet of 6 short-stemmed yellow tea roses: "Hi. I've been remiss in not thanking you until now for the lovely shawl which you boxed so expertly. My grandmother was absolutely taken with it. Please accept the flowers as part of my apology and my thanks."

Lysa felt her throat tighten and her heart flip-flopping against her rib cage but she returned his smile and said, "No need to apologize. It's my pleasure when someone enjoys the items that I sell. I'm not really sure I should accept your flowers after all, you did pay for the shawl."

He laughed warmly and added, "Well, I did have an altruistic reason for bringing them. I would like to invite you to have dinner with me tomorrow night if you are free. I can pick you up here or if you prefer I can pick you up at your home."

Lysa hesitated. "I don't know you. I don't generally go out with people I don't know."

The man laughed warmly again. "I don't normally ask a woman out to dinner if I don't know her either, but somehow I kept thinking about you after I had left the store. I've been away on business; else I would have come back sooner." He took a card from his wallet and gave it to Lysa with one hand while holding out his other to shake hers. "My name is Adolf and this is my business card. Please take it. If you don't want me to take you out tomorrow, just call me. Otherwise I will pick you up here at 6:30 to give you time to do whatever needs doing after you close at 6:00; or, as I said earlier I can pick you up at your home at a different time if that is more convenient for you."

Lysa looked at the card he had handed to her: Pfeiffer Pharmaceuticals; Adolf Stone, pharmaceutical representative. A cell phone number was printed in blue font at the bottom of the card. She looked back at Adolf, shook his outstretched hand and said, "I'm pleased to meet you Adolf. My name is Lysa Brighton and I will think about your invitation and give you a call either way." It felt very business-like but Lysa was not about to give into the butterflies that seemed to have invaded not only her stomach but every cell in her body.

Adolf shook her hand with a firm grip. Thanked her and walked out the door.

"I may not be home for dinner tomorrow night mom" said Lysa as she and her mother sat down for their evening meal. "I had a dinner invitation from a one-time customer today and I'm debating about whether I will accept."

Her mother waited for Lysa to continue and by waiting she was rewarded with the full story of the tall slender stranger. "So he has left you feeling a little out of breath, has he?" her mother quipped good-naturedly. "So why not explore that feeling over a dinner? Seems to me that you've got a better chance at deciding where you want to go with this encounter when you are sitting across the table from one another, talking, than you have ruminating about what he makes you feel while you hide in your store."

"You're probably right mom" Lysa replied slowly and then added, "no; not probably. You are right mom. I will call him tomorrow and let him pick me up at the store. I've got his business card; I've seen him twice now. It's better than internet dating."

They had both laughed and spent the remaining evening in pleasant conversations about the store, family memories and silly imaginings about Lysa finally having a serious man in her life. "What would dad say about him?" was the last question her mom had asked. It was more of a statement; an imperative measuring stick for a potential suitor.

Lysa interrupted her musings and took another sip of tea. She wondered why she had never followed her mother's imperative. Her father had been a good judge of character. "Integrity, Lysa" he would say, "integrity of character is everything. What a person says and does must be congruent. How you treat someone even when you think no one is watching says a lot about you, dear heart. It's more than just politeness, more than just political correctness, more than just the right words at significant times—it's how you behave towards people whether they are strangers or your closest friend; it's how you treat people who are weaker than you; it's being honest even when it means that there are consequences that hurt for a short while; it's showing your true colours as the commercial says. I hope that I have lived like that, pumpkin; I know your mom has. That's what we want for you."

Had she been true to herself that morning when she phoned the number on the business card? "This is the voice mail of Adolph Stone. Please leave me a message."

"Hi Adolph. This is Lysa. I will go to dinner this evening with you. You may pick me up at the store at 6:30 as you suggested. Have a good day."

She had only briefly wondered why the answering machine message had not identified him as the pharmaceutical representative of Pfeiffer Pharmaceuticals but then told herself that he probably used the same phone for both personal and business calls and therefore kept the message succinct. Her dad might have asked "But is it honest? Is it transparent?" But she had failed to ask those questions or perhaps more correctly had pushed those questions aside. She was satisfied with her interpretation. "What difference would it have made anyway?" She shrugged her shoulders and sipped her tea as she mused about her reaction to the phone message that day. "It probably would have made no difference. Dad wasn't around to talk about it and I probably wouldn't have said anything to dad in any case. It was what it was."

For a moment Lysa halted her memories. "Of course," she said out loud, "why didn't I see that before? I'm a pragmatic. So often I've told myself, 'it is what it is'. I allowed some of the things to happen in both our courtship and our marriage because I simply believed that is what life is about and there was nothing I could do to change things. What a fool I am. How could I ever have been so single-minded and clear headed when it came to business and so blind and besotted when it came to love? Is that what love is—being blind to your own perceptions about the lover? Do we agree to be trapped into decisions and behaviors that we would shake our heads about if we were to observe them in someone else? Why do we make excuse after excuse for the inexcusable behaviours of our lover? Why do we accept apologies and excuses that we know are meaningless? Why? Why? Why?"

Lysa felt her blood pressure rise, her temples pounding and hit the table with her hand making the dishes she had piled up rattle, "Yes," she heard herself shout out loud, "I am glad to go down memory lane tonight. There will be no pragmatism when he charges through that door. I don't have to accept his drunkenness or his abuse. I can't change his past but as sure as my name is Lysa, I can change my future." She closed her eyes, inhaled deeply and saw her father grinning at her the way he used to when she was in grade school. "Lysa," he'd chuckle, someday you'll drive me crazy with all your 'why's. Some things just don't have an easy answer." "Yah dad," she said out loud, "but sometimes you have to ask the 'why's' and keep digging so that you never make the same mistake again. It's what I'm doing now dad. I need to know how I got into this mess so that if I get out alive tonight I will never make the same mistakes again." She sighed heavily, took a long sip of her tea and returned to her memories.

It was busy day; more so because it was Caroline's, her shop assistant, day off. So, when Lysa finally locked the door to the store she would have preferred to just go home, put on her slippers and curl up in bed with a good book. She went into the washroom at the back of the store, splashed water on her face, brushed her teeth and ran a comb through her hair. "I guess I`m as ready for this date as I'll ever be" she thought as she put on a light jacket and slung her bag over her back. She set the store alarm and went out the front door, locking it behind her; then stood for a moment to decide what she might do next. It was just after 6:30 and except for a few people on the sidewalks and several cars driving by the street was empty. She waited another ten minutes before she started to make her way towards the bus stop to go home when a car drove up beside her and honked. She looked and saw the now familiar smiling face. He waved at her to get in as he apologized for being late. "Sorry Lysa. I was held up by a client. And you know that the client is always right—even when he isn't." He laughed his good-natured laugh as she got in and buckled the seat belt.

"I'm glad you didn't leave right away. I would have been most upset with myself if I had missed you," he continued. "I've booked a table at the Mayberry House. I hope you will like it."

The Mayberry House had once been a stately mansion overlooking Brandy Inlet. It was sold a few years ago and was now considered one of the top restaurants in the city. Lysa was taken aback. Her business attire would be conspicuous among the clientele of Mayberry. She was about to protest but felt that he may be hurt by her comments. It seemed evident that he was trying to impress her so she just said, "Thank you. I am sure I will like it. I have read a number of great reviews about the restaurant."

The evening had been magical. The table by the window provided a magnificent view of the sunset and later of the millions of lights of the city below them. The food was superb. She had ordered the fresh crab cakes served with fingerling potatoes, a medley of roasted spring vegetables and a piquant arugula and mustard green salad. Adolf had ordered a rose Pinot Grigio to accompany their dinner. They spoke of his work. Adolf had hoped to enter medicine after graduating from school but in grade 11 his father found work in Oregon and Adolf stayed with his grandmother with whom he and his father had lived after his grandfather died. He said he could not remember his mother; she had a nervous breakdown when he was a toddler and left him and his father. They never saw her again as far as he knew, and he had never had the inclination to search for her. His grandmother was a wonderful caregiver and it was obvious by the way he spoke of her that Adolf was very fond of her, but the departure of his father left him feeling abandoned. His marks slipped and by the second year at university, he realized that he would not be able to compete with the students who were vying to enter medicine. In his third year he applied for and was accepted into the school of pharmacy which became his degree. He could not see himself working in a pharmacy so when he received an offer to become a pharmaceutical representative, he took the position. He said it fulfilled most of his desires—travel, meeting with doctors and researchers, a good income, and a fair degree of freedom to plan his time.

Lysa in turn told him about her life, growing up here in the city, the only child of George and Elizabeth Brighton. Her father was a welder and had worked for the Brigton shipyards for as long as Lysa could remember. Her mother had been a primary school teacher. Once Lysa had entered school her mother worked half time so that she could be home when Lysa came home. It was a cheerful household. Her mother encouraged Lysa to bring home friends so that the evening meals would frequently see two or three youngsters around the dining table regaling her mom and dad with their adventures and antics. Many of the friendships had been maintained over the years and Lysa had enjoyed their support in the months following her father's death and the opening of her business. The girls she had grown up with were her cheerleaders, her clients and her dearest critics. Without their frankness Lysa might have made some serious mistakes in the first year of her store. Her effusiveness about her friends seemed to puzzle Adolf as he struggled with trying to tell Lysa about what might have been friendships for him in his school years. By the time that they had finished their bottle of wine followed by coffee and a light fruit soufflé, three hours had passed. Adolf drove her home and walked her to the door. She had lightly kissed him on the cheek and thanked him for a delightful evening. He thanked her, asked if he could call on her again and after she said "yes" he left.

Over the next several months, Adolf had taken her out to the symphony, a football game, a movie and several more dinners. She enjoyed his eclectic interests but became aware that he did not seem passionate about anything outside his work. He had avoided speaking about friends after their first date and when Lysa had suggested that they get together for Thanksgiving with his grandmother and her mother, he had simply stated that he was on a road trip for several weeks and wouldn't be back for the holiday. Had her dad been alive he might have questioned whether Lysa was overlooking something, but her dad was dead and Lysa was in love.

At Christmas Lysa invited Adolf and his grandmother to their house for Christmas dinner. While her own immediate family consisted of only her mom and herself, Christmas always saw her mother's brother and his wife as well as her four grandparents around the dinner table. Adolf had initially declined the invitation but two days before Christmas had phoned to say that he and his grandmother would be delighted to come. Once all the introductions had been made, the evening was a most congenial affair.

Adolf's grandmother, Henricke, was short in stature and slim like her grandson. She had flaxen colored hair that was cut short and softly curled around her face tempering the strong cheek and chin bones that spoke of a northern European heritage. Her eyes were clear and blue-grey in color. She, like Adolf, spoke with a firm, cultured tone like someone who had voice training or experience in public speaking. Warmth radiated from her face as she greeted Lysa and met the members of her family. While Adolf seemed uneasy in a family gathering, Henricke was very much at ease in the group. Lysa liked her immediately.

Lysa began to visit Henricke regularly, especially when Adolf was out of town. The two women could speak more freely without

Adolf in the mix. While Adolf rarely spoke to Lysa about his childhood and in those rare moments when he did, remained vague in his recollections, Henricke began to unfold the difficult story of his life. Henricke was the mother of Adolf's father, Rudolf, a man who, in her opinion was filled with anger and unresolved emotional issues stemming from her husband's cold and demanding parenting style and her own failure to soften those demands.

"My husband spent a good portion of his childhood in boarding schools and thus learned little when it came to be a parent. His own father was emotionally unavailable, and as result, my husband was emotionally unavailable to his son. He believed that children do best in a strict environment. Rudolf could never really measure up to my husband's expectations of the boy and as such they never had a genuine connection."

It was not that Adolf's grandfather was abusive—he never hit the boy—he was simply cold and emotionally unavailable to Rudolf just as his father had been to him. While she had tried her best to soften the edges of her husband's relationship with his son, Rudolf became increasingly rebellious and eventually cut all ties with his family. He married young.

"And the girl he married was also too young and not strong enough to respond to Rudolf's demands for obedience and his harsh reprisals when she failed to live up to his standards." Henricke shook her head in sadness. "Rudolf directed all the anger he had for his dad towards that poor little girl he married. His demands on her were similar to the demands that his dad had made of him while he lived at home, only" Henricke drew in a sharp breath, "my husband was not a physical man like Rudolf became."

The birth of Adolf was the beginning of the end. Adolf was colicky as an infant and very hyper-active as a toddler. To Henricke's best knowledge, when the boy was about three years of age, Rudolf had beaten his wife while he was in a drunken rage to the point where she had to be hospitalized. The neighbours had called the police and an ambulance took her away. She never returned. Henricke's eyes filled with tears as she spoke about this time. It was evident that she bore the guilt of not knowing what happened, the guilt of not being able to help, heavily and was glad that she had someone now in her life in whom she was able to confide.

Rudolf received custody of the boy and for several years seemed to take a genuine interest in Adolf's well-being. While he would not allow his own father to see Adolf, Rudolf found opportunities to occasionally meet with Henricke so that she could get to know her grandson. When Adolf was five, Henricke's husband died and Rudolf and Adolf came to live with her. The honeymoon period of having her son back under her roof was short lived. Rudolph began to drink more heavily; he became a womanizer and spoke disrespectfully of the women who he would bring home. Longer relationships always ended in women leaving as Rudolf would physically and emotionally abuse them but in all this, he made no demands on his son in the manner that his own father had done.

"It was his saving grace" said Henricke. "Rudolf loved Adolf but because he had not experienced a healthy father-son relationship, he tended to relate to Adolf more as a peer than a parent. I would occasionally try to tell Rudolf that he should not speak about women in front of the boy but then Rudolf would get angry and tell me that I had no right to tell him how to parent since I had not interfered with the way my husband parented him. He had a point of course. I tried to protect Rudolf from the criticism of his father, but I can honestly say I didn't speak to my husband about his relationship with the boy."

Henricke would shrug helplessly as her stories unfolded. "Adolf adored his father and did not connect emotionally to any of the women Rudolf brought home. On the contrary, Adolf believed that his father was right treating women with disdain because his mother had also left them. I tried to explain that his mother had loved him but had a breakdown and couldn't cope with the demands of being a wife and a mother, but a boy will believe his father over his grandmother."

When Adolf was just entering his teen years, his father got a job in Kurland and had asked Henricke to look after his son. He came home periodically but the times in between became longer and the visits shorter. He provided materially for Adolf but, except for the visits, made no contact with his son.

"In time, the only thing that they had in common when Rudolf did visit, was their mutual disdain for women and Adolph`s pursuit of the sciences" said Henricke. "In a way Rudolph had become the father that he had loathed—emotionally unavailable to his son."

Henricke would often sit quietly for a time reflecting on the story that she entrusted to Lysa but at each visit she would add more details. "Perhaps there was a difference between my husband and our son and the relationship Rudolf had with Adolf. While Rudolf could do no right in his father's eyes, Adolf could do no wrong in Rudolf's eyes. Rudolf would praise his son's achievements in school and encouraged him to become a doctor. In turn, Adolf did his best to work hard in school and showed his father his report cards and annual achievement awards when his father visited. In many ways, I had a lot of hope for both men although, to be honest, I was glad that Rudolf was not around a lot. If nothing else, through Rudolf's absence, I was able to give some balance to Adolf's opinion of women. He at least made a connection with me and always respected me."

When Adolf was in his second year at university, his father died after a bar fight. Adolf drove to Kurland to arrange for a cremation and returned with the few meager belongings from his dad; belongings that he carefully packed into a small wooden box with hammered brass hinges and a brass lock; the box he and his dad had made years ago when Adolf was eight years old. Adolf returned to university, but it was obvious to Henricke that something had died inside the boy. While he had always been quiet and a loner, he was even quieter and kept to himself more than before. He did not appear to have either male or female friends. His evenings at home were spent studying and at the end of each year he would apply to go tree planting, a job that took him into the wilderness. Henricke thought that these summer months away helped Adolf heal. At the end of each summer, he returned home, tanned, fit and in a lighter mood that quickly changed with the advent of classes.

And so it came as a surprise to Henricke that after graduating with his degree, Adolf decided to accept the job of a pharmaceutical representative. It seemed incongruent to his personality. However, the past five years had proven Henricke's concerns wrong. Adolf had become very successful in his career. He regularly won top sales awards and was recognized by his company with increasingly larger territories and financial incentives. "And now," Henricke would look long and hard at Lysa before she continued, "it seemed that he has fallen in love."

Lysa would come away from these visits with a heavy heart. How could this beautiful, old woman, have carried such a heavy burden alone? And the question at the end of each visit would weigh on her: 'What was she to think about the tortured legacy that had shaped the life of the man with whom she had fallen in love? And how much did she really know him outside of what his grandmother had told her? Would it have made a difference if she had waited longer before marrying Adolf? Would her head knowledge about what might happen in a marriage have overridden her heart?"

Lysa shrugged away the questions she couldn't answer even now, rose from the table where she had been sitting, stretched herself and walked to the window. She knew that he wasn't close to coming home; she needed to look down the long driveway flanked by the slender Lombardy poplar trees that reminded her of an era of horse and carriage, long sweeping skirts and men with top hats. It could have been so beautiful—her life, his life—here. She had loved to work in the garden planting rhododendrons and azaleas in every variety of color. Adolf remembered how she had taken him to the Elmwood Gardens in Victory when the rhododendrons were in bloom and how she had told him that if she ever had a garden that is what she would plant. On their first wedding anniversary a truck from the local nursery arrived with ten beautiful bushes ready to be planted. She shivered unexpectedly. "You can't go there Lysa; you can't go back. If you go down that road tonight you'll be lost," she scolded herself, turned abruptly and sat down in her chair facing the door.

"You are the veritable romantic, Lysa," she said to herself. "That's why you thought that nothing would touch the two of you after you were married. That's why you thought that Adolf's life was a sad story that you could change. So now you've identified two of your weaknesses—pragmatic and romantic. O.K. girl, what's next?" Lysa smiled as she chided herself in the plural as if there were two Lysas in the room, the Lysa who was telling the story and the Lysa who listened and confronted her. She poured more tea into her cup and continued unpacking her memories.

It was July 10 when Adolf asked her to marry him; a year and a month after they had their first date. He had phoned her the day before from Bellaire and asked if she would like to spend the evening with him when he got home the following day. She had teased him and told him she would have to check her diary first. They had agreed that he would pick her up at the store and go to a comedy club for dinner that was followed by an improve-theater performance. They had gone to the club twice before and found the food to be excellent and the performances hilarious. Lysa chose a flirty chiffon dress from her wardrobe, matched it with a pair of small-heeled shoes and a light seersucker jacket in anticipation of an overenthusiastically air-conditioned dining room. Adolf had already parked the car outside the store when she finally locked up and went to meet him. He enfolded her in his arms, kissed her gently and told her he had missed her. Lysa returned his embrace and kiss and for a moment they simply enjoyed being together again.

The theatre was just starting to fill when they arrived providing them with the opportunity to be seated near the stage. The menu was a west-coast fusion of American-Japanese food—fresh seafood and amazing local vegetables and fruits. Adolf ordered a bottle of champagne. "Did you get a promotion today?" she had asked. His usual dinner choice was a Pinot Grigio or a Merlot. Adolf's eyes sparkled, "No. I'm just glad to be here with you tonight and that is enough reason to celebrate." And for a while, they just sat, holding hands across the table: lovers comfortable with the sweet silent presence of one another. The waiter interrupted them to pour the champagne and ask if they would like to order. Adolf asked him to bring a bowl of fresh salted edamame while they looked over the menu.

As was the custom in the theatre, one of the young actors came to our table to give us each a piece of paper and a pen. Customers were encouraged to write down a title for a scenario which would become part of the evening's program. It surprised Lysa to see Adolf write something on his paper and fold it, ready to be picked up. He had never participated in the past although she had always written something--not that it had been used. Lysa smiled, "Care to let me in on this one?" Adolf grinned back at her. "If they choose it, you'll know. If they don't I'll let you know later."

They ordered their dinners and munched on the edamame, sipped their champagne and talked about their week at work. Lysa felt comfortable with this man although they seemed to have so little in common outside their passion for their work. Yes, they were both only children and both worked hard to achieve their current professional success but that is where the similarities seemed to end. Adolf was charming, attentive to her, engaged in their conversations but it seemed that outside his work he had little interest in people or the world in general. Lysa knew that she had neglected some of her friendships while she was at school and starting her business, but she kept in touch and would periodically take time to hike the local mountains or go kayaking up Indian Arm with her long-time friend Lynda. How often had she heard her dad ask on a Saturday morning, "And where are the 'Ells" off to today?" 'The Ells', was her dad's favorite nickname for her and her friend as they chummed through high school and into college. Lysa also knew that she had neglected some of her interests, but she still found time to putter in the garden and sit at the piano to entertain her mother with songs from her past and to read a wide variety of books. Most of her creative bent was now focused in and on her store, in the selection of her items, in the displays, in the seasonal decorations and in the artistic website she had developed and updated regularly. "Perhaps work was mainly what life at their age was about," she had mused.

Lysa had probed Adolf on numerous occasions about his friends and interests but he was as vague about those as he was in his discussions of his childhood and youth. They had double-dated once with Lynda and her husband George. Lysa had suggested they go bowling and since none of them bowled regularly believed that it would be a fun evening. They met in the lounge off the bowling alley for cocktails and a light dinner before bowling. It had gone well. Adolf had charmed Lynda immediately and had shown an interest in George's work as brew master in one of Grange Island's cottage breweries. But the bowling was a disaster. Lysa was totally taken aback by Adolf's competitive spirit. Instead of an evening of laughter as they rolled gutter balls or created impossible splits, Adolf became increasingly agitated with every ball he rolled until at the end of the first game he turned to Lysa and said angrily "This is not for me. I'm out of here. Let George and Lynda give you a ride home." And without looking back to say good-bye he grabbed his shoes and stormed off. Lysa had shrugged at her friends in utter amazement, "Guess this wasn't such a good idea after all. I better see if I can make sense out of this with him. Sorry guys. George grinned at her, "We'll do something that doesn't involve games next time." They bid Lysa good-bye and she went to search out Adolf.

She found him in the car with his hands gripping the steering wheel and his head slumped over the wheel. "Are you O.K.?" she asked quietly as she got into the car and tried to put her hand on his arm. He shook the hand off violently and turned to her, his face still contorted in anger, "Don't you ever put me in that kind of situation again. I will not be made a fool of especially not in front of a bunch of strangers."

"I'm sorry. I certainly didn't mean to make a fool of you. I thought we would have fun since none of us are bowlers." Lysa tried to keep her voice low and even to avoid agitating Adolf more.

"There weren't just four of us non-bowlers there. There were serious bowlers there. I saw them eye us. As far as they were concerned, we had no business there and I totally agree."

"It wasn't a league evening, so we had every right to be there," Lysa raised her voice to match Adolf's tone, "and if they wanted to eye us so what? What we do for our entertainment is none of their business. We aren't judging them. Why would they judge us? They're playing their game; we have ours."

Adolf took his hand off the wheel and grabbed her arm. It hurt. He swung around in his seat to face her directly and hissed, "All I'm saying Lysa is don't ever put me in a position like that again. Do you understand?" She nodded silently, and he let go. And rather than pursue what to Lysa seemed an over-the-top response to what strangers might think of them, she also let it go. It seemed easier. She grimaced as she remembered that evening. She had put it down to being a peace-maker but in retrospect Lysa knew that she had given in because she didn't know how to handle confrontation. "Perhaps that is what pragmatism is", she mused, "the inability to deal effectively with the ugly bits of life so you just let it go and shrug it off."

Lysa's gut knotted at the memory and she feigned a smile at Adolph sitting across the table from her this evening writing something on the paper that the actor had given them, folding it and passing it back to the actor. After the actors had collected the papers from the various tables they would choose several as the theme for their impromptu skits for the evening. Lysa drew a deep breath and hoped that Adolph's idea would not be chosen.

"Penny for your thoughts; or maybe I should say 'nickel for your thoughts' since we don't deal in pennies anymore." Adolf's voice was soft and kind. "You were miles away and I would like to be with you on that planet."

She laughed uneasily and lied, "I guess I was just thinking about the sea urchins that gave up their life to feed us tonight." She reached for his hand and poured out her heart, "Adolf, I love you so much; sometimes it frightens me how much I love you. I'm no princess but I long for a fairy tale ending—to live happily ever after."

"You are my princess," he said softly, took her hand to his lips and kissed it.

"Ladies and gentlemen, thank you for giving us great skits for tonight. The titles were truly creative, and we want to start out with one that really caught our attention called "A modest proposal". It just had to be created by some guy who has no idea on how to get laid. I mean who would ever be so timid? We think that this guy needs a few lessons in how to throw out a line to a lady." The actor had everyone in stitches. It would be a naughty skit.

He made his way over to a table filled with young men and women. "O.K. Let's hear it from the women. What kind of a line would make you fall into the arms of a timid man with a modest proposal?"

There was a lot of laughter and giggling before the answers came: "You cast a spell on me. Whenever I look at you everyone else disappears." "Will you come to my church? Because you are the answer to all my prayers." "Can I check you out? Someone seems to have stolen my heart and I hope it's in your possession." The lines and laughter went on as the men had a turn to try their wits. A voice from the back of the room shouted, "You're a princess. Want to sit on my throne?" Lysa sucked in her breath and felt herself blush. That had been very close to home. She avoided looking at Adolf by intently cleaning the empty bowl of tiramisu with her spoon. Had someone overheard the tender words that Adolf had just recently spoken to her and used it as a joke? She swallowed hard, regained her composure and laughed at the next line without really having heard it.

The actor had wound his way around the room until he was at their table. He looked at Adolf, "Well, she is absolutely delectable, isn't she? What is your modest proposal now that you've been primed with all the lines from the audience?" Lysa turned beet red—Adolf had given him the title to this skit. Was he going to play along and embarrass her tonight or would he just get up and leave? She stared as almost with one motion, his hand disappeared into his jacket pocket producing a small box at the same time falling to his knees in front of her chair. "Lysa, my darling, will you marry me?" He had flipped open the box holding the most beautiful diamond ring that she had ever seen. The room filled with shouts, and hoots and applause. People by their table stood up and clapped their hands. The actor had stopped in his tracks and now held the mike in Lysa's direction. "Oh yes, yes, yes, yes I will". Tears flowed from Lysa's eyes as her voice crescendoed her acceptance and the noise and clapping in the room almost overwhelmed the actor's last comment "Now that is what I call a truly modest line. It sounded like she already invited him to bed just listening to him." The place exploded in hoots and laughter. Adolf rose from the floor, took Lysa by the hand and giving the waiter an envelope, they left the theater.

It had taken an amazing amount of courage and Lysa often recalled that moment when his anger flared. "A Jekyll and Hyde. What made him so? How could anyone be so courageous in their announcement of love on the one hand be so vile and hurtful months later? How could a princess become a harlot overnight?"

Lysa looked out of the window. It was very dark now. There were no street lights along the lane that led to their house. She felt the tears course down her face and thought that she would like to pray. But how do you pray after you had turned your back on God? As a child Lysa had gone to Sunday school and at age 14 she was confirmed in her church. Her parents were not religious, but they would attend church at Christmas and Easter and they attended her confirmation. After that there seemed little point in attending churches except for the holidays, much more a cultural experience than a religious one, and even that had been left behind when she married Adolf. She tried to remember some of the prayers she had learned at Sunday school but drew a blank. "Where are you God?" she shouted, looking towards the ceiling in desperate anger. "If you can hear, why don't you help me?" She threw her cup at the door and watched it break. "Let it stay," she said angrily, "maybe when he comes home, he'll grind it to pieces with his feet like he ground me to pieces. That would be a fitting start to our encounter tonight."

"If I'm going to get through my memories before he comes, I had better stop thinking about God and prayer and concentrate on what I must remember before I face my final hours with him. It's too late for God." Lysa chose another cup from the set of china Henricke had given them and filled it with tea. She held the cup lovingly in both hands. "I'm so sorry Henricke, there is nothing I could do either. Adolf has become his dad. He will continue to hurt me and anyone else who is stupid enough to love him in the future. It wasn't that I wasn't forewarned. You told me everything. I guess I just didn't want to hear the warning."

Lysa shook her head, had she heard it or remembered it: "they have ears but don't hear; eyes but don't see." "So what good does that do me now God?" she looked up at her ceiling as if expecting to see some apparition stare down at her with a look that said, "I warned you."

"Oh sure; you warned me. You gave me Henricke but she loved him too. So what good was that? Why didn't you just strike him dead; or me dead? Why did you have to take Henricke and leave me alone with him? Why drag me through this inferno? What good does that do to you?"

Lysa looked back down to the cup in her hands. She had clenched the cup so tightly that the rings on her fingers hurt her. Carefully she put down the cup and removed the rings from her fingers, placed them to the right of the knives and thought about the symbolism of her action. She was cutting herself free from her husband, her tormentor.

"But when and how did she know that she had made a mistake? When did her prince turn into the beast she had lived with these past several years?" Lysa thought back to the fairy-tale time between her engagement and the wedding. She could not have felt more loved; not have loved more deeply. Their routine remained the same; Adolf would be away all week—sometimes ten days—and would take her out to dinner when he returned. They went dancing on several occasions and took in theatre performances and movies. They did not return to the dinner-theatre where he had proposed.

On Sunday afternoons they most often visited with her mom and later in the evening with Henricke. They spent long hours walking the sea walk and talking about where they might live after the wedding and how they would balance their work life with their married life. They set a date for early summer when the west coast is awash with color. They both wanted a simple wedding inviting only the closest friends and family. It would be a civil wedding with the ceremony and the dinner located at the Vancity Golf Club. Lysa told him that she had asked Lynda to be her bridesmaid and George to walk her down the aisle. She asked him if he had someone in mind who would be his groomsman, but he always had a reason why he hadn't asked someone.

As the time grew closer, Lysa asked him for his guest list. Adolf had again been vague and when she pressed him to finalize the numbers for the Golf club, he became angry at her. "Pick a number yourself. I have no idea who I'm going to invite. This was supposed to be a small event but since you decided to orchestrate it, just leave me out of it" he shouted, walked out of the store and slammed the door. Later in the week he phoned her to apologize. "I'm sorry Lysa. I know that you're doing your best to create a memorable day for us, and somehow, I don't really get it or maybe don't really feel part of what is happening. I guess tradition has it that the bride's family puts on the wedding, but I'm not used to people telling me what to do. I like to be in charge," he laughed, "but here it is, I`ve invited my boss Jim Shore to be my best man and he will bring his wife Audrey. Besides them only my grandmother is on my list."

In the weeks before the wedding Adolf had been out of town a lot and when they had time together they spoke little about wedding plans. Adolf said that he would be happy with whatever she planned as he trusted her taste. She asked if he would wear a light grey suit as it was spring, and she would order yellow tea roses for the lapels for the men and the corsages for the women. She would carry a small posie made of yellow tea roses and white baby`s breath. She showed him the menu for the dinner and invited him to choose the wine which he declined to do, saying that the caterer would be in a better position to pair it with the menu. Lysa smiled wryly as she recalled the time he had phoned to give her the guest list; it seemed that since he felt he wasn't in charge he would not participate in any manner. Still the wedding had been a wonderful affair. She had purchased an ankle-length chiffon dress in pale ecru with a matching beaded jacket and a broad brimmed hat. Lynda had worn a teal blue ankle length dress. A limousine picked up her mother, Lynda, George and herself and drove them to the golf course where they met Adolf, his grandmother and his boss and wife. Adolf and Jim wore silver grey tuxedos with teal blue cummerbunds—he had been listening to her prattle after all. The evening could not have been better. Adolf had again charmed Lynda and George as well as his boss Jim and Audrey. He was a most attentive groom who had made her feel the princess that he had said she was the night of the engagement, and a most magnanimous grandson and son-in-law. A limousine drove the guests home and a second limousine drove them to the Martin airport hotel where they spent the night before flying to Sandio and driving to Moon Bay where they spent a week honeymooning.

Looking back, Lysa thought she could see that the cracks in the honeymoon that had now become the gulf that lay between them. It had been easy to sit and talk over food or to go on a walk when they were dating and seeing each other at intervals; it was different now that they spent all day and night in one another's company.

Adolf was a great lover and Lysa learned to explore his body with the same passion that he explored hers. "You are the most beautiful woman I have ever lain with" breathed Adolf into her ear the first night at Moon Bay. She had held him tight and answered, "you are the only man I have ever lain with and I couldn't imagine ever lying with anyone else." He pulled her close and kissed her hard so that it hurt, "I think I would kill anyone who tried it on with you," he breathed, then let her go and gently stroked her face and hair. "I will never share you with anyone, Lysa. I have never loved anyone the way I love you. Sometimes it frightens me how much I love you." His voice was low with an edge that sent a chill down Lysa's body. If he felt it, he made no comment.

Lysa reflected on the remaining honeymoon which, had she not been so much in love, might have raised small flags for her. Adolf ensured that the two were always alone. They did not participate in the new-comer luncheon, games evening or pool-side events. They walked the beaches, swam, ate at a table for two and made love. He seemed oblivious to the beauty around him and shielded her from engaging in conversations with staff or guests by simply walking away with her or answering for her in a curt manner that made it clear that conversation was not wanted. And on the occasion where she suggested that they join in a game of beach volleyball, he firmly but quietly declined. "This is our time, Lysa, we need to get to know one another, not a bunch of strangers." It seemed logical.

Adolf suggested that they move into his house just outside of Bellaire. It was a beautiful two-story house on a five-acre property with a large front garden that she had always dreamed about. Lysa had concerns about commuting each day to Vancity but Adolf suggested that she could have Caroline look after the shop and to eliminate the long commute she could continue to live with her mother when he was travelling or when Caroline had days off. While Lysa would have preferred that they rent a studio suite close to her shop, she could see that keeping two households made little financial sense and the charm of the house and garden was irresistible. As such the life in the first year of her marriage was much like the two years of courtship with Adolf travelling and she in the shop except for those days when Adolf was at home. Lysa promoted Caroline to manager so that she could share some of the responsibilities of managing the shop when she was in Bellaire and hired a second shop girl to assist when either she or Caroline were absent. Caroline created a web-page for on-line shopping which increased the revenue of the shop markedly. Caroline brought additional skills to the shop including the creation of a blog to which both Caroline and Lysa contributed writing articles about up-coming fashion trends, features on local designers and general information about clothing and accessories. Life seemed idyllic.

Although Lysa occasionally spent time at the house, the visits were short-lived, and she did not make the effort to meet with the neighbours whose homes were nestled about half a mile down each direction of the country road. She still felt much more at home in her mother's house. Still, she spoke to Adolf about having their families come to Bellaire for Christmas. It would be her first opportunity to really make the house feel like a home. Adolf took time off from work a week before Christmas and told her he would be home until after the new year. Lysa would drive to Bellaire Christmas eve after she closed the shop early and the two would have the evening alone. Her mom, her uncle and aunt and Henricke would drive down Christmas day and stay with them for a couple of nights.

Prior to her coming, Adolf had used his time off to decorate their home. She was smitten by the rustic adornments he had used to beautify the home inside and out. Adolf had hung a large evergreen swag adorned with soap berries and holly from each of the posts to the entrance of the house. In the living room he had set up an 8-foot spruce tree lit with tiny white bulbs and decorated with silver pine-cones. Pots of poinsettias were clustered by the large stone fire-place that burned cheerily as she entered. White candles wrapped in white birch bark gave light to a dining table that he had set for the two of them. She smelled the spiced wine simmering on the stove and pork loin baking in the oven. Adolf had waited for her just inside the front door and was pleased with her response to all he had done, "Wow. I had no idea that you were gifted in interior decorating as well, dear heart. Every time I turn around I find out something more amazing about my talented husband." She threw her arms around him and held him tightly to her.

Christmas could not have been better. They had a pleasant visit, a sumptuous dinner with their guests and spent the days playing card and board games. After their guests had left, Adolf dismantled the decorations, and although Lysa was disappointed to see everything come down, she also knew that she could not do it by herself after he left on January 2. They were invited to a New Year's Eve party by one of the neighbours, but Adolf declined the invitation wanting to spend the first new year alone with his bride.

Winter rolled into spring. Lysa spent most of her time at her mother's place, going down to Bellaire only when Adolf was at home, so she was excited and looked forward to her time at the house to celebrate their first anniversary and was thrilled to work in the garden. Lysa thought she might create a vegetable garden as well as an herb garden this year and get a good feel for the property, much of which had been left in its natural state with large evergreens and wild, rambling bushes. Only the front of the property had been somewhat cultivated with a large lawn flanked by flower beds that had been overtaken by weeds and the beautiful driveway with the Lombardy poplars that created a grand entrance to their home.

She had decided to take a month holiday, working only on her website and blog, and leaving the management of the store to Caroline. The week prior to their anniversary, Lysa had devoted to cleaning out the flower beds and making a list of plants that she wanted to purchase when Adolf came home. She decided that flowering bushes were the best choice as they required little on-going maintenance and would eventually create a peaceful garden setting that they could enjoy in every season. Her first choice was rhododendrons and azaleas which would provide color from early spring to early summer. For summer colours she decided on salal, a low growing ground cover with small flowers in spring and berries in the summer and early fall, dogwood, yarrow and mock orange; and for late summer and fall colours she chose red elderberry and purple leafed Japanese dwarf maple. She would discuss spacing and clustering with a local gardener so that the plants would have sufficient space to mature and create the picture she had in her mind. In the center of the garden, as a focal point, Lysa wanted to plant a blue spruce which to her was one of the most beautiful trees in God`s creation.

She was surprised how much she felt at peace as she puttered in the garden enjoying the beautiful solitude of their home. Adolf said he would arrive home about 4:00 p.m. on their anniversary. It was only 10:00 a.m when she heard a vehicle driving up the driveway. Lysa brushed the flour from her hands that had been creating pastry shells for the quiches she wanted to serve at their evening meal. A young man sprang out of the cab and met her at the front door. We have a delivery for Mrs. Stone. Could you please come out and tell us where you want us to plant 10 rhododendron bushes? Lysa could hardly contain herself and foolishly babbled “who ordered those?” She knew it had to be Adolf before the young man could reply, “Mr. Stone.” Lysa showed the men where each bush was to be placed and continued to ramble at the older man who mixed the soil while the young man dug the holes, “It’s our first anniversary today. Isn’t this the most amazing anniversary gift that you could imagine?” The older man smiled. “Yup. He must surely love you a lot. These aren’t cheap you know.” They were finished at noon and Lysa went to fetch a couple of glasses and cold lemonade which they gratefully accepted. She gave each man $50. The older man told her that everything was paid for but Lysa insisted on giving them a tip. They had done an amazing job and had even watered each of the plants before cleaning up and loading the garden debris that they had dug up while planting the bushes. She waved good-bye, went back to the kitchen to complete making the quiches and then showered and changed into a skort with matching halter top. She wanted to knock Adolf’s socks off as he had knocked off hers with this astonishing gift.

It was shortly after four o'clock when Adolf drove up the driveway. Lysa stood by the open door and ran to the car to meet him. Adolf swept her into his arms and kissed her, then still holding her looked at her and said, "Wow! Now that is an anniversary present." Lysa laughed and took him by the arm, "I have something to show you." She walked with him to the center of their front yard and pointed to the newly planted rhododendrons, "I couldn't believe it when the truck drove up this morning and the young man said, "I have a delivery for Mrs. Stone from Mr. Stone." She put her arm around Adolf's waist, "The most beautiful thing about this gift was that it came from a passing comment I made to you when we had visited Elmwood Gardens in Victory even before we were in a serious relationship." Adolf pulled her close, "I was serious about you from the day I walked into your shop to buy the shawl for my grandmother." They kissed and then walked hand in hand back to the car where Adolf took out his suitcase before heading back to the house.

Lysa popped the quiches into the oven and tossed a mixed salad while Adolf unpacked his things upstairs. When she heard him coming down, she opened a chilled bottle of chardonnay and poured two glasses. Adolf took the glass from her and said, "How sweet and kind were you to the young man who came with the bushes?" Lysa grinned and teased, "As sweet as anyone would be to a young, pimply faced boy barely out of high school." Adolf's voice became cold, "Yea, I bet he got an eye full". Lysa continued to be light and laughed "I detect little horns growing on my husband's forehead." Adolf grabbed her arm tightly so that she winced, "I don't want my wife parading around men like some tart." Lysa was totally taken aback, "A minute ago I was a delectable sight and now I look like a tart? I dressed up especially for you" she said bitterly, "let me go. You are hurting me."

Adolf released his grip. "I'm sorry. I guess I did feel jealous that anyone would see you like this. Tell me that you weren't dressed like this when the delivery was made."

"I was making pastry when the truck came. What do you think I was wearing?" Lysa was hurt and the hurt was obvious both in her look and her voice.

Adolf apologized, "I am truly sorry. I should have known. I just love you too much to share you with anyone. Can we start over?" The oven timer allowed Lysa to turn around and attend to the baking and think about what he had said. She put on her oven mitts, opened the oven doors and took out the quiches. She placed them on a cooling rack. Yes, she knew what she wanted to do. Removing her oven mitts, she turned back to Adolf, picked up her glass, leaned over to clink his and smiled at him, "We'll start over." The evening was as magical as Lysa had envisioned it and the incident long forgotten as Lysa lay in his arms.

At breakfast next morning Lysa asked Adolf if he would enjoy hosting a neighbourhood barbecue the following Saturday. He grinned and asked, "Where did this come from?" Lysa explained that she had been mowing the lawn on Tuesday when a pick-up truck stopped in front of the property and a man stepped out to hail her. He told her his name was Bob and that he and his wife Elizabeth were our next-door neighbours on the right. He said it was nice that new people had moved into the house as no one ever saw the previous owner. "It was a little creepy" he concluded. Well Lysa had to laugh. She said that the new owner was the very same elusive owner he talked about. It was just between his job and his courting her that he was seldom here. Now that they were married they would be here more regularly. Bob had suggested that perhaps they could get together and Lysa had replied that she would run it by her husband who would be home on Friday.

Adolf had listened to Lysa's story without comment or without visible change in his facial appearance. She had expected a rebuff and was almost taken aback when Adolf said "Well, since you seemed to get the ball rolling perhaps we should go ahead and host a barbecue. It might be nice not to be considered 'creepy' by our neighbours." Adolf laughed. Lysa grinned, "O.K. do you want to call them, or shall I?" "I'll call them" he said. "They can bring their own meats and whatever they drink and we'll supply the salads, buns, and dessert. How does that sound to you?" "Perfect." Lysa replied.

The rest of the week had a honeymoon feel to it for Lysa. They took walks around the neighbourhood, left an invitation for the new neighbours who were not home but appeared to be moving in, puttered in the garden, shopped for the Barbecue and made the dessert and salads. Adolf seemed to enjoy preparing food and tried out his hand at barbecuing several times that week. He even purchased himself an apron for Saturday that said "Wanna-be Master Chef". Life for Lysa seemed faultless.

On Friday, Bob and Elizabeth were the first to arrive. They introduced themselves to Lysa and Adolf who shook Bob's hand warmly and laughed "I'm the creepy guy who lives in the house."

They both laughed and let Elizabeth, who was looking very puzzled, in on the joke. Adolf took the steaks that Bob held out to him and put them into the cooler, Elizabeth handed Lysa a bottle of wine, saying, "Let's open it now and share it. I specifically cooled it so that it would be perfect for a before dinner drink. I hope you like Pinot Grigio. "We love it" Adolf and Lysa said almost in unity. Lysa went to bring out wine glasses and a wine cooler while Adolf and the guests chatted.

Wendy and Gerry, the couple that was moving into the house across the street arrived just as Lysa was pouring the wine. They introduced themselves as "Ma and Pa Kettle". Wendy was very much pregnant, and their last name was indeed Kettle. "When we are not practicing being mom and pop, I'm Gerry and my wife is Wendy." More laughter and another round of shaking hands ended with Lysa asking Wendy if she would like a sparkling apple juice, a fruit punch or water. Wendy chose the fruit punch and Gerry said he would like a glass of the sparkling apple juice as he wanted to support Wendy's abstinence in alcohol during her pregnancy. Lysa ducked into the house to get the beverages and returned to hear Elizabeth ask how long Gerry and Wendy had been married. "We've been married five years" said Wendy. "Gerry is an aero-space engineer and works at the plant outside of Seattle in their design department. We lived there in an apartment. I'm a primary school teacher. When I got pregnant we decided that we would like to raise our children in a rural setting. Gerry can work from home for part of the week and then drive to Seattle for a couple of days. We kept our apartment, so he has a home away from home. We were very lucky to get this place. Gerry's dad knew the couple, Mr. and Mrs. Brown, who owned it and had asked them some years ago if he could buy it if they ever decided to leave. Mrs. Brown had a stroke earlier this year and they decided that it would be better if they lived closer to Seattle for her treatments, so they called Gerry's dad. By this time his dad and mom really didn't want to move from their place, so he asked Gerry if we would like to buy it. Gerry jumped at the chance and I am over the moon. It is perfect for us. We want to get a horse and a dog along with children." Wendy patted her stomach and smiled, "We are having twins. This is going to be a great place for a family."

The chuckles and affirmations were interrupted by the sound of a truck pulling up at the front of the house. "That must be the Johnsons," said Adolf, as he put down his glass and went to meet them. The third neighbours had arrived. Mike, a tall, burly man in his early seventies was accompanied by his wife Mary whose smiling face could have lit up a neighbourhood. “Hello, hello,” she beamed holding out her hand to greet Wendy. “We haven’t had young people in the neighbourhood for ages,” she turned to Lysa and smiled, “and now we have two new young couples at the same time.” She gave Lysa a warm hug, “thank you for organizing this soiree”. Mike introduced himself to Wendy and Gerry and then greeted Bob and Elizabeth before giving Lysa an equally warm hug. Adolf followed Mike carrying a large box. “I think the Johnsons wanted to make sure that we could party for a week,” he laughed. “Just a couple of steaks and whatever you drink, we said, and here Mike comes pulling out a box of groceries from the truck.”

“Hey, you don’t know Mike yet,” quipped Bob, “he’s got a big appetite.” Rounds of laughter continued with light conversation as Adolf lit the barbecue and Lysa began to set out plates, salads and poured more wine and juice.

Elizabeth told us that she and Bob were celebrating their thirtieth wedding anniversary this coming fall, and Bob had said that they would go on a second honeymoon to Belize. She laughed and added, "our first honeymoon was a week-end camping trip. We wouldn't have known what Belize was unless it was something to eat. We were as poor as the proverbial church mice when we first started out, but Bob was a man of many talents and I had a good job as a nurse in Bellaire. We decided that Bob would go into business, so our first big expense was a back-hoe; there was always a need for someone to get something dug up. Later we bought a truck and Bob was able to expand his business by hauling stuff. We bought our little farm down the road twenty years ago. By that time, we had two little ankle-biters running around a very small apartment. It was the best move we ever made," and smiling lovingly at Mary, she added, "so I know that your move will bless you in the same way, Mary."

Over steaks and salads Lysa learned that Mike and Wendy were old-timers in the valley. Wendy's parents owned the farm where they now lived. They had been vegetable farmers who supplied the green grocers in the area. Wendy grew up loving the farm but was not so keen on the work required to grow vegetables. When Mike came along to work one summer as a farm hand while attending Washington University for a degree in animal husbandry, Wendy became enamored with both—Mike and the idea of raising animals. Wendy gave her husband a warm smile and said, “Fortunately the feeling was mutual.” Mike grinned, “I couldn’t believe my luck—a beauty and a farm. Wendy’s parents had planned to sell the farm when they retired but with a farm-hand in the family they decided that we could buy them out over time as long as they were able to live with us. No hardship there. Mom and dad Simmons were as easy going as their daughter and we had built-in connections to the community when we decided to raise goats and make cheese instead of continuing to grow vegetables.”

It was close to midnight by the time everyone had a chance to talk about themselves and their hopes and dreams for the future. The evening had been a smashing success by Lysa’s account and she continued to chatter on animated by the conversations as she and Adolf cleared the dishes and put away the left-overs. She had become aware that Adolf was quieter than usual and put her hand on his arm, “Getting tired darling?”

He pulled her hand away by the wrist and holding it tightly turned to face her and hiss, “Don’t darling me, darling; not after your shameless flirting with Bob who just lapped it up while his poor wife and I had to watch.”

Lysa looked squarely into his face, "Let go. I have no idea what you are talking about. Just tell me what I did that made you think I was flirting."

"Don't pretend you don't know" Adolf hissed again, "then the close-up hug saying good-bye was all that I needed."

Lysa continued to stand and look at her husband without flinching. She lowered her voice and put an edge to it to match his, "No I don't know, Mr. Stone, and I gave everyone a hug as they left. I felt that they had all been so open, sharing their lives with strangers, that there was no reason to think anything except how grateful I was that they were our neighbours. I'm sorry if that offended you. I thought you had as good a time as I did." With that Lysa turned around and saying goodnight, walked upstairs to their bedroom.

Lysa stopped her memories to recall that moment. She had been strong then. She had set boundaries on what she would accept as his behaviors. When did she become so weak, so fearful of this man?

It felt like a long night after Lysa had left her husband downstairs and had gone to bed. Adolf did not come to bed and she struggled with what to do. Part of her wanted to go and beg him to forget the evening and part of her wanted him to know that she would never betray his love but would also remain true to herself. By the time six o'clock arrived she could no longer remain in bed. Lysa showered and put on her jeans and a t-shirt and went downstairs. Adolf was stretched out on the couch, his clothes and shoes still on, a small afghan pulled over his chest and arms. He looked so vulnerable in his sleep. Lysa tiptoed to the couch, bent over his head and kissed him lightly on the mouth. "Oh Adolf, I missed you so much in bed last night. Let's not fight. I can't stand it when we are not O.K. with each other."

Adolf reached up to touch her face. "I'm sorry too, Lysa. I get so jealous and then I didn't want to go to bed with you partly because I wanted to punish you but also partly because I wasn't sure whether you would want me."

Lysa lowered herself on top of Adolf and whispered, "I will always want you Adolf."

Lysa closed her eyes now as she recalled the passionate love-making that seemed to follow every fight they had. She had held her own in the first couple of years, not giving into his anger or his jealous accusations, until exhausted they would make love and make up. "Like a couple of stupid teenagers" Lysa muttered to herself and sat awhile sipping her tea until the cup was drained. She placed it carefully on the saucer and sighed. In the end he had won. When did she stop fighting with him? When did love-making turn into something that she once would have called rape?

It was the end of July when Lysa and Adolf again made time to be together in their home. Lysa's garden was taking shape and Adolf had a load of fire-wood delivered that he wanted to chop for their fire-place in the winter and stack in a small lean-to that seemed to be built for just that purpose. They had finished breakfast when Elizabeth called. "Hi Adolf, is Lysa around?" Adolf handed the phone to Lysa raising his eye brows quizzically as he did so. He could see the surprised look on Lysa's face and hear the joy in her voice. "Did you?" "Yes, yes, we do that." "Of course, I can. See you in about an hour. I'll just clean up here and I'll be over. Bye."

Before he could ask, Lysa told Adolf that Elizabeth had seen the web-site from her store and read her blog. She wanted Lysa to come over to her place and help her plan a wardrobe for Belize. Bob had said that she could get some new things for the trip and since Lysa was in the business, Elizabeth wanted her to do the outfitting. Adolf had said something about inviting Elizabeth over to their place but Lysa said she needed to look through Elizabeth's closet to get some idea of what she already had and what she might need. "I'll be back around lunch. Call me if you need anything," and giving her husband a kiss, Lysa grabbed her bag and was out the door.

It was less than an hour later when Adolf called. "Come home right away, Lysa. Something has happened to my grandmother and we need to drive to Vancity General. Henrike was taken to the hospital by ambulance. Lysa shivered as she hung up, told Elizabeth what had happened and promised to be back later in the week to finish planning the wardrobe.

The drive to Vancity had been a silent vigil. Lysa prayed silently that all would be well with Henrike as she saw the hard lines on Adolf's face and his fingers clutched tightly to the steering wheel, the speedometer relentlessly above the posted limit. They swung into the Nexus lane at the border and were at the hospital in just over an hour after leaving home. They parked in the emergency parking lot and Lysa told Adolf to go ahead; she would deal with the parking ticket and meet him in the ICU.

By the time she arrived, Adolf was sitting at the bedside holding his grandmother's hand, silently weeping. Henrike opened her eyes as Lysa walked in and whispered, "Thank you". Turning to Adolf, she whispered "I love you. Look after her." Then closing her eyes, she was gone. Bells rang, nurses rushed in, monitors were inspected, she and Adolf were pushed away, but it was all for naught. Henrike died. They watched the nurses cover her face. Adolf gave them his cell number and said he would contact the funeral home to come and take her body and then they walked silently out of the hospital to the car. Lysa put her hand on his arm. Adolf looked at her with empty eyes and said, "I'm taking you to your mom's place; I need to be alone." He gently shook her hand off his arm, put the car into gear and drove wordlessly until they reached her mother's home. "I'll call you when I've made all the arrangements." His voice was cold and lifeless. He didn't wait for a reply, "Please get out now. I need to be alone." Lysa stepped out of the car, and almost before she had time to close the car door he drove off.

Lysa ran into the house, into her mom's arms sobbing. Little by little she told her mom what had happened, not just to Henrike but Adolf's reaction to his grandmother's death. "I know he was close to her, but I loved her too, mom. It's like he cut me off. I have no idea what he's doing and even less how to help him."

Her mom held Lysa until her sobs had subsided. "Adolf asked you to leave him some space just now Lysa. Allow him to grieve. Call him tomorrow if he hasn't called you and then ask how you can be of help."

Lysa did not sleep that night. She grieved the loss of Henricke and the absence of Adolf. She wanted to comfort him and in doing so be comforted by him. Her emotions ran from anger to helplessness that continued to dissolve into tears.

Lysa held herself back from calling him the next morning until 9:00 a.m. Her call went to voice-mail. She texted him asking that he call her. There was no response. She went to the store to relieve her frustrations and anxieties but found herself calling or texting almost every hour. Soon after lunch she left Caroline to care of the store and went for a long walk. Her grief had now morphed into anger against her husband. An hour later she found herself standing in front of Henricke's house. She walked up to the front door and banged ferociously. There was no answer. She waited, put her ear to the door: no sound. Was he there? She tried to peer through the window by the door but saw only the empty hallway.

Slowly she turned and walked another hour to her mother's house. She was exhausted—not so much from the walking as from her emotions. She briefly greeted her mom, went to the bathroom, filled the tub with hot water and a lavender bath salt, shed her clothes and bathed until the water was almost cold and her fatigue prompted her to go to bed. She fell almost immediately into a deep sleep and did not wake until early next morning.

The night's rest had its desired effect: Lysa felt stronger. She dressed, went downstairs to make herself a coffee and called Adolf's cell. This time she left a message to let him know she was feeling better and would like to see him. She made breakfast for herself and her mother and then left for the store. Lysa did not call or text although occasionally she was tempted to do so. He wanted space; she would give him space.

Thursday morning, she called him again and again left a voice mail. She could feel anger tickle the back of her throat. "How insensitive and self-centered could any person be?" she questioned. Lysa went to her store but the anger that had tickled her throat in the morning, began to close in on her chest as noon approached. By lunch time she told Caroline that she would be gone the rest of the day. She would see Adolf today whether he liked it or not.

Lysa drove up to Henricke's house and knocked on the door again. There was no answer. She tried the door; it was locked. She went around to the back of the house, up several steps to a porch that lead to the kitchen and tried the door. It was open. She crossed the porch in three steps and tried the kitchen door; it was also open. She entered, quietly closed the door behind her and listened for sounds; the house was eerily quiet. Slowly Lysa went through the kitchen, the dining room and living room. Nothing had been touched. It was as if Henricke had just gone out for the day. Lysa walked down the hall and up the stairs to where the bedrooms were. The door to Henricke's bedroom was open but nothing had been touched. She turned, walked down the small hall to where Adolf's bedroom was. The door was closed. She opened it carefully and looked in. Adolf was sprawled across the bed, his clothes still on, empty bottles of liquor everywhere. The room smelled like a drunk tank at a police station. Lysa wondered about her analogy since she had never been in a police station let alone a drunk tank—"One of those stupid sayings we pick up and toss around even when they don't mean anything", she thought. She strode across the room to open a window, picked up the bottles and placed them by the door and then sat herself by the lifeless looking body of her husband. She stroked his hair that felt greasy from sweat and bent down to kiss the side of his face letting her own tears erase all the anger she had felt about his behavior towards her. It really was different for him. He lost the person who had been his mother after his own mother had abandoned him. He felt abandoned once again. He had drunk himself into a stupor to forget.

Lysa went to the washroom, took a clean facecloth from the cupboard, wet it with warm water and returned to wash her husband's face. She went back and forth several times. It was on the fourth time when she put the warm cloth on his face that he turned, opened his eyes and hissed, "I told you I needed my space. Get out of here." Lysa repressed the anger that surfaced again and answered quietly, "I was worried about you. You didn't reply to my calls or my texts. And I found you here in a drunken stupor. It looks like you've been drinking since you left me at mom's place on Tuesday. I know that you are sad..."

Adolf sat up with a jerk. His face was contorted in anger and his voice was threatening, "Get out! You know nothing. This has nothing to do with you. It's my problem and I've got to deal with it. So just leave."

Lysa put her hand on his, "You are my husband so it's also my problem. I loved Henricke too and must deal with that. I'm not leaving. I love you and I think we need each other."

That was the first time Adolf raped her. When he was finished, he got up, zipped up his pants, and turning to go out he said in a flat even voice, "You are just like all the tarts I had. It's all about you. Have a good day." And then he was gone.

Lysa lay on the bed for what seemed like hours, tears gently streaming from her face, wetting her hair and the pillow where her head rested. She tried to make sense about what had happened, but nothing came to her. Slowly she dressed herself and left the house to drive home. She was glad that her mom wasn't in and went upstairs to the bathroom where she dropped her clothes and showered, shampooing her hair repeatedly until her arms were tired. She dried herself, wrapped a towel around her and went to her bedroom to dress. Then she returned to the bathroom, took her clothes and the towels she had used and threw them all into the washing machine.

Hearing her mom, she went downstairs and said "Hi mom. Let's go out for dinner tonight so we don't have to clean up. I'm tired and can't think about cleaning anything else."

Restaurant conversations tend to be surface which was just what Lysa had hoped for. She told her mom that she had seen Adolf that day and that he had been drinking and that's why he didn't really want her around. It seemed logical and it somehow quietened the violation and fear that battled in her gut. Her mom responded with warmth so that Lysa began to feel safe again although she could not bring herself to talk about what had happened between her and Adolf. She wasn't even sure that what she thought had occurred. How could a husband rape his wife? It was the drink. It was the pain of losing Henricke. It was…

Lysa looked down at the cup that she held in her hands which had begun to sweat as she remembered that day. She carefully put down the cup and ran her hands down her hips to dry off the sweat and to distract herself from the tears that threatened to well up and spill over. She had made so many excuses for her husband over these short five years. She needed to take ownership of each excuse, of each time she swallowed her pride to be the wife she believed Adolf needed, of each time she kept silent or lied about what he did. She had to take responsibility as much as he had to take responsibility. Without that she would not be able to say the things that she needed to say to him tonight when he came home.

She remembered now how he called her Friday morning and asked if he could see her about 10:00. They could have coffee together at the little cafe just around the corner from her shop. His voice was quiet and conciliatory. He said that he knew he had hurt her with his behavior and wanted to apologize. Lysa agreed to meet him.

He was already sitting at a table with two cups of coffee and two pastries when Lysa arrived. He greeted her, and she simply said "hi" and sat down. Adolf reached for her hand as she reached for the cup. She did not move. "I'm sorry Lysa. I have been a jerk. Please hear me out." He remembered the rape differently from what she experienced and emphasized her words that she needed him as much as he needed her. He was glad that she had come when she did, but he still had so much anger in him about Henricke's death that he took it out on her. He apologized for his remarks after they had sex and asked her to forgive him. He withdrew his hands from hers and took a sip of his coffee. Then, looking directly at her he grimaced and said, "Perhaps grandma was right when she said we take our anger out on people we love because we can feel safe with them."

Had he just been venting anger? Lysa swallowed the sadness that had been left by that encounter and accepted his story as an attempt at an apology. Bending her head down towards the untouched pastry, she quietly had told him that she was still hurting but that she would forgive him.

They drank their coffees and ate their pastries in silence before Adolf asked if she could help him clear Henricke's things so that they could be donated to a charity. Anything that Lysa might like to keep, she could.

It took about a week for Lysa to sort through Henricke's clothes and jewelry. She washed, ironed, and packed the clothes for the charity shop. She sorted through the jewelry and kept aside pieces that had sentimental value for her and gave some pieces to Adolf that she thought he may want to keep. He was not around much during that week but would appear with lunch baskets or coffee and pastries that they would share at the kitchen table downstairs. Lysa tried, on several occasions, to bring up stories about Henricke, but Adolf would shut her down. He did not wish to talk about his grandmother.

Lysa inquired about a memorial service but Adolf did not even entertain the thought. He had placed an obituary in the local paper and had honored his grandmother's wishes to be cremated and the urn placed in the ossuary with her husband's urn. He did say that if Lysa wanted to have a tea for Henricke's friends the following week that she was free to do so. He would be back at work then and would probably not see her again for a couple of weeks. He would leave the keys to the house.

Lysa had met some of Henricke's friends. The following week she began to phone them using Henricke's address book and invited them to an open-house tea in Henricke's home on Sunday afternoon. A stream of people came and brought flowers and cards and asked about Adolf. Lysa was tactful and vague letting them know that Adolf had to return to work. Still, it was at least somewhat of a closure for Lysa. She needed to see Henricke's life honored and in turn was given treasures of stories about her wonderful "grandmother-in-law" from the people who had know Henricke for so many years.

The rhythm of life had changed. Lysa felt alone and isolated herself increasingly at the house in Bellaire working on designing a new line of clothing and leaving the day-to-day management of her business to Caroline. She visited with Elizabeth and put together an elegant wardrobe for the "thirty years later honeymoon". It was safer to be with Elizabeth than with her mother. Elizabeth was bubbly and excited about her upcoming trip and had been satisfied with a brief description of Henricke's death and Adolf's difficulty dealing with that loss. Lysa knew that if she continued living at home and going to her shop that she would break and tell her mom about the rape. Her heart knew it was rape; her mind tried to rationalize what had happened. She felt wounded and yet scolded herself for forcing Adolf to share his grief with her. "What happened was my own fault" she would say to herself, "so deal with it or let it go."

Adolf would come for the week-ends. He would help her in the garden and cook the dinners but aside from superficial conversation they did not talk. Love-making had changed to sex and often Lysa felt as if she were the prostitute that he had called her that day—she felt nothing.

Lysa went home for Thanksgiving. Adolf said he wasn't free that week-end and encouraged her to spend time with her mom. Lysa had learned to be "breezy" and while her mom noticed the difference in her daughter, she was unable to push past the wall that Lysa had carefully constructed to protect her vulnerable self. But a week at her mom's and in her shop was all that Lysa could manage and she returned home.

Christmas was not the exciting time it had been the year before. Lysa had decorated the house early and then returned to Vancity for the busy buying season in the shop. Her mom, aunt and uncle came back to Bellaire with her late Christmas eve to stay until after Boxing Day. Adolf had made a welcoming fire in the fireplace and had set a table of assorted meats and cheeses, breads and sweets and had created a warm Norwegian grog. For the first time in months, Lysa had felt warmth return to her soul. It was a pleasant evening and when they had retired, Adolf had held her gently until she melted into his body. They had made love again.

The remaining holidays were tenuous for Lysa; it was as if she were walking on thin ice hoping that it wouldn't break—that she wouldn't break. Slowly she re-connected emotionally with her husband. She began to talk about her growing on-line business, her ideas about designing clothes, and her thoughts about selling a portion of her store to Caroline. Adolf seemed interested and encouraged her especially in the sale of the store. They accepted Elizabeth's and Bob's invitation for New Year's Eve and enjoyed their stories and pictures from Belize with Elizabeth frequently pointing to an outfit that Lysa had provided. They bid their friends good-night after midnight and let them know that they would probably not be around during the month of January.

New Year's day, Adolf told Lysa that he would be on a road trip for about three weeks but wouldn't mind taking a week's holiday after that. He needed some alone time and hoped she wouldn't mind. Lysa felt hurt but simply said it would be okay as she was going to be busy talking her business ideas over with Caroline and if all went well there would be lawyer appointments to keep her busy.

She was glad that she had business to keep her mind occupied. Caroline was excited to enter into a genuine partnership with Lysa. They divided the business with each owning 50% although their working arrangement would remain much the same. Caroline would look after the day to day in-store business and continue to help Lysa update their web-site; Lysa would look after the on-line business, assist with the web-site, write the blog and work on her own clothing designs which they would sell exclusively in their store. Lysa found a small clothing manufacturing company that would take her designs and sew them.

January had passed more quickly than Lysa had imagined but was ready to return home to Bellaire to normalize her life again. She re-decorated one of the bedrooms into an office complete with computer, printer, sewing machine, professional dress form mannequin and fabrics. The planning, the physical work and the organizing kept the dark thoughts at the back of her mind, slowly allowing them to take a shape she could live with—the shape of a broken man who needed her unconditional love to heal; the shape of a woman who would forgive and forget all the pain to rescue her husband from himself.

Adolph arrived the first week-end in February. He had not phoned her in advance. She wondered if it had been on purpose; if he wanted to catch her by surprise like a parent watching a child to catch them doing something wrong. She had brushed the thought from her mind and greeted him lovingly. They made dinner together and spent the evening catching one another up on their respective work over the past month. Lysa had shown him how she had changed the spare bedroom adjoining their own room upstairs into her working office. Adolph seemed impressed but asked why she hadn't taken the office downstairs as her work room. She said it was his office and as he didn't protest the comment, she felt that she had made the correct decision. They spent the week-end in casual conversations, shopping and watching television. What should have been a relaxing time left Lysa on edge always wondering if the veneer of comfort would suddenly break under the tension to reveal the ugly heaving creatures that inhabited both their souls.

Before he left for work again, Adolph asked her if she would like to go for a four-day retreat at Paradise Inn in Florida that coincided with Valentine's Day. His boss had reserved six rooms for himself and five of his top sales people. The business meetings would be held for two hours each morning and the remainder of the day would be free for them to spend as they wished. "In any case," Adolph added, "it will be nice for you to get away from the cold and damp this time of the year to somewhere warm."

It was the warmth in his voice when he asked her to go that melted the unease she had felt all week-end and she was able to respond with honest excitement. “That sounds absolutely wonderful, Adolph.” He seemed relieved and assured her that he would arrange the flight and be home a few days earlier to help her with anything that needed to be done around the house before they left. Lysa burst out laughing, “Thanks. I will love to have you at home early, but there is really not much that needs doing before we leave.” He swept her into his arms, kissed her good-bye dissolving the tension that had lain between them yet once again.

Lysa was excited. She packed a light pant suit, several tops, a skirt and jacket, bathing suit and several soft shawls. Four days to re-connect with her husband. Four days to completely melt away all the pain and darkness that had stuck to her since Henricke’s death. Four days of warmth inside and out. It was impossible to keep to herself. She phoned Elizabeth, Caroline and her mom—in that order—to let them know of the wonderful Valentine’s treat Adolph had surprised her with.

The holiday was everything Lysa could have hoped for. They enjoyed breakfast with the other guests before Adolph went for his two-hour meeting. Lysa took the time to take a book to the outdoor patio and let the sun soak its warmth into her bones. When he was finished, Adolph would bring her a coffee, stretch out on the chaise next to her and chat to her about the meeting. They would change into light slacks, t-shirts and walking shoes and walk to town for lunch and a couple of hours of browsing before heading back to the hotel and their room where they napped and made love. Unlike previous holidays, Adolph arranged to meet one or more couples from the company for dinner each evening. He was charming, attentive and relaxed. By the last evening, Lysa believed that they had finally put the past nine months behind them; that life would become easier.

Her hopes were short lived. Back in Bellaire, Adolph announced that he would be gone for two weeks. When Lysa stated that she would also be away from home for ten days to manage the store while Caroline went to Montreal to participate in the fall and winter fashion shows for buyers, Adolph struck his hand on the table and shouted, "What was the point of dividing the work when you go off to Vancity at the drop of a hat? This house is a mess. I come home, and you have jobs lined up for me that you should have done so I can have a break. You wanted to be married then start acting like a wife." He strode out the door and slammed it behind him.

It was late when Adolph returned home. He had been drinking. Lysa had gone to bed worried and felt relieved when she heard his footsteps on the stairs. She sat up when he came into the room and said, "I've been worried about you." Adolph did not answer. He shed his clothes on the floor and forced himself on her. Lysa had not struggled. She let him take her while compelling her thoughts back to the four days of love-making and letting the tears run freely down her face.

He rolled off her. "I'm leaving early. Do whatever you want but be back here when I get back. I've had enough of having to share your time with everyone you please while you neglect me."

Lysa had simply answered, "I'll be here. Be safe." She rolled onto her side, buried her face in her pillow and sobbed herself silently to sleep.

He was gone before she got up. Lysa packed her things for the ten days she would be at her mother's place. She stripped the bed and put on fresh sheets as if she could wash the hurt away when she put the bedding into the washer. She cleaned the kitchen and scrubbed the floor. When he returned this time, the place would be impeccable. Only after she was totally satisfied that things were spotless, did Lysa set the alarm, lock the door and drive off.

She was glad to be full-time in the store, talking to her customers, creating new window displays, going over the books with her accountant and meeting with the seamstress who would turn her designs into samples for the manufacturer. It was more difficult to spend time with her mom. She spoke glowingly about the four days away but was vague about the days before or after the holidays. Part of Lysa wanted to confide in her mom but another part believed that she would be betraying Adolph if she did. She felt trapped in her own thoughts.

Looking back, Lysa thought that this was the moment when fear began to replace the love she had vowed to have and hold for the rest of her life. She had returned home reluctantly two days before she expected Adolph. She struggled with her thoughts, wanting to hold on to the warm feelings he had engendered in her while wondering how he would treat her when he returned home. Would he be pleased with how the house looked? Could she give him the rest that he needed after two weeks on the road?

Should she talk about what happened before he left or pretend that all was well with her?

It was dusk when she turned into their driveway and saw his car parked in front of the house. Her heart raced, and her throat closed so that she could barely breathe. Before she had time to think about what to say, he was out the front door, walking quickly towards her car. She shut off the engine as he opened her door and waited for her to step out the car. He enclosed her with both his arms and whispered "I am so glad to see you. I was so upset with myself after I had left you without even saying goodbye that I was worried you wouldn't come home." He held her, kissing her face and hair murmuring over and over, "I'm sorry Lysa. I love you." Lysa melted into his arms, the hurt and the worry dissolving like snowflakes on a child's tongue. As he helped her unpack the car and bring her things inside, she had chided herself for worrying.

Adolph had dinner prepared and complimented her on how lovely the house looked when he got home. She patted herself silently on her back for the work she had done before leaving. "Yes. She could be a wife," and vowed to make every effort to please him in the future. It was worth it.

Over the next six weeks, Lysa enjoyed being at home. Adolph had only short trips away with two or three days at home between trips. Their time together was spent gardening, shopping, cooking. Adolph joined her doing the things that seemed to have upset him earlier. Lysa asked nothing of him; it was Adolph who asked her how he could help. He had accepted invitations to dinner twice in the six weeks, once from the Johsons who were delighted to show them the new born goats. By the time Adolph and Lysa got home, they knew more about goats and their kids—yup, that is what their babies are called--than they had ever wanted to know. And yet, the evening had been exceptional. Lysa saw her husband in a new light as he listened and queered Mary and Mike about the habits and diets of goats. Mary had prepared a feast of a Philippine goat stew called caldereta, which she served with garden vegetables and rice. Adolph asked if they sold their goat meat and when Mike said, "only to friends and family", Adolph had grinned and said "Then I hope you will count us as friends."

The second invitation came from the Kettles. Lysa talked to Wendy the week before they went for dinner stating that she might have the touch of the flu as she was experiencing some nausea but had no other symptoms. Wendy had laughed good naturedly and said “Sounds like you might be pregnant. Wouldn’t that be exciting. Our kids could play together, go to school together....” Lysa interrupted her with a laugh, “Woa, woa! Don’t get ahead of yourself. I think I just have a light touch of the flu. If I don’t feel better by Saturday, I’ll let you know and we’ll take a rain-check for dinner.”

Lysa’s heart pounded after hanging up. She wanted so much to know if her nausea signalled that she was pregnant or if it was, as she had believed up to this moment, the flu. The nausea did not stop but neither did it become worse and she went to dinner.

The evening was delightful with the twins entertaining them with toddler antics until Wendy said it was time for bed. Lysa asked if she could help tuck them in while the men had some time to talk about things other than babies. Wendy raised her eyebrows quizzically but said she’d be glad for the help. While the two women put the twins into their pyjamas, Wendy asked Lysa how she was doing. Lysa confessed that the nausea had not abated but was too nervous to get a pregnancy test or make an appointment with the doctor. She also didn’t want to speak to Adolph yet since they hadn’t even discussed whether he wanted a family or not. Wendy shrugged, “Some men can be funny about things like that. They don't want to share their wives with anyone including children." Lysa had nodded quietly as she recalled the vehemence in Adolph's voice when he told her he wouldn't share her with anyone. "Yeah. Maybe I'll get that doctor's appointment first. I mean once it's a fact, there is little else except to get used to the idea. And he didn't seem to mind the twins at all." She looked at Wendy as she tucked the blanket over the wiggly body and added, "I'll let you know when I know." Wendy put her arms around Lysa and hugged her, "I'll be with you all the way. Take your time. Get the test when you are ready and let Adolph know when you are ready." Wendy's compassionate tone seemed to find a crack in Lysa's carefully crafted defenses. It was as if Wendy knew that Lysa's life was not all that she tried to portray.

Dinner had the amicable feel of a budding friendship for both the men and the women and when Adolph and Lysa finally bid their hosts good-night, Adolph suggested that they invite the couple for dinner soon. He had enjoyed Gerry's talk about work at the aeronautics' plant in Seattle and believed that in some respect both men had work in common—spending time away from home. Lysa's attempt to talk about the twins was lightly brushed off and she did not pursue it. She had an ally—Wendy—and that was all that she needed right now.

Adolph declined an invitation from Bob and Elizabeth with the excuse that they were taking in a movie in Bellaire with a couple from work. Lysa had raised her eyebrows and Adolph had shrugged, "I don't want to spend another boring evening listening to them replay the details of their trip."

"So, what do you want to do that evening?" Lysa asked. "We can't just hang around the house when they expect us to be out."

"Well, if they want to snoop around to see whether were gone or not, they're more than welcome to do it. Maybe they'll get the hint that I really don't care about their invitation." Lysa held her tongue; Adolph's voice had the edge that she began to recognize, the edge that meant another word would end up in a blow—metaphoric or real.

But as the evening in question arrived, Adolph suggested that they go for dinner. He wanted to try out a new Thai restaurant along Samish Way overlooking Lake Samish that he had read about in the Bellaire tourist Trip Advisor. Lysa gave her husband a hug. Life was beginning to feel good.

She believed that she had become the wife he wanted and as long as she was able to read his moods and respond appropriately, he was the husband that she thought she could live with. It wasn't perfect, not like the courtship, but "don't all marriages have their hiccups?" she would ask herself. "And didn't all people have their idiosyncratic behaviours that a couple had to work out over time?" After all, hadn't she insisted on the right side of the bed because she had always slept on the right side; and didn't he just laugh it off and allow her to have that side? "Yes, it will take us time to round off the rough edges on both of us. It is the way marriage is." And yet she was unable to bring herself to let her husband know she was pregnant. She had made the appointment the week following dinner with the Kettles and had received the results the week after. Maybe this evening, after dinner, she would tell him that she was pregnant—had been pregnant for almost three months. His Valentine present to her would be her early anniversary present to him.

It was the Victoria Day long week-end for Canadians and traffic in Bellaire was busy. Adolph had made reservations for 7:00 p.m. but suggested that they leave early and take a walk in Big Rock park before dinner as the weather was warm and the rhododendrons would still be in full bloom. The park had been filled with visitors taking pictures of the stunning rhodos, flowers and sculptures but for Lysa the whole park might have been vacant except for the man whose warm arm encircled her waist as they walked the well-groomed paths.

It was obvious by the crowded parking lot that the restaurant was popular. They were unable to secure a table near the windows as their reservations had been made late, the hostess explained as she lead them to a lovely little table on a small balcony. Adolph said to her, as she gave them the menu, that the view was perfect, caressing Lysa's cheek across the table as he spoke. He had a moment of dissonance on his face when he wanted to order wine and Lysa declined saying that she was on a cleanse and that alcohol was to be avoided. She chose a sparkling cranberry soda instead. Adolph had shrugged but had not pressed the issue. Lysa couldn't remember what they had ordered that night, but only remembered the romantic warmth between them punctuated by warm laughter as they tried to feed each other a shared dessert.

By the time the car drove into their drive-way, Lysa had made up her mind that tonight would be the night she would tell Adolph about becoming a father.

"Come upstairs with me, darling," she said and reached for his hand after he had closed the front door, "I have a surprise for you."

Adolph had looked at her quizzically but followed her upstairs without a word. "Come to my work room." Lysa opened the door and lead him in. There on a dressmaker form, Lysa had pinned a stylish maternity dress. "What do you think?" she asked. Adolph shrugged, "I guess there will always be a market for maternity clothes."

"Do you like it?" she continued? "I really don't have an opinion on women's clothing especially pregnant women's clothing."

Lysa took a deep breath, took Adolph's hand and put it on the small bump that had formed in her abdomen, "You may want to start having an opinion."

Adolph's hand flew away from her belly as if it had been placed on a hot stove. "What are you saying, Lysa?" His voice was icy.

Lysa looked at him and quietly said, "I'm pregnant, Adolph—three months now. It happened on our Valentine's week."

"You dirty piece of garbage" he shouted. His hand crashed into the side of her face so that she stumbled against her cutting table, and before she could steady herself, he shouted again "I have a vasectomy. This creature is not mine," and the second blow landed on the other side of her face so that she fell to the floor. She rolled into a ball to protect her belly and her face as he kicked her again and again shouting the invectives that hit her heart as intensely as his shoes hit her body: "You harlot! You Jezebel! You lying piece of garbage!" until she passed out.

When she regained consciousness, the room was dark and empty. Adolph had left and had shut off the lights and closed the door. Her head and ribs and hips hurt as she slowly started to sit up. She listened. There was no sound. She tried standing but felt nauseous and sat down again and pulling the small quilt that she had started to sew from the cutting table, she made herself and little pillow and lay down to wait until day.

She must have dropped off to sleep because the next time she woke the sun was streaming through the window. She listened. There was still no sound in the house. Slowly she pulled herself off the floor into a standing position and took several deep breaths before she dared to walk to the door and open it a crack. There was no noise. Lysa walked into the hallway and peeked into their bedroom. The bed had not been slept in. She walked to the head of the stairs and listened. There were no sounds coming from downstairs.

She returned to their bedroom, closed the door behind her and propped a chair against the door. Only then did she feel safe enough to strip off her clothes and go into the bathroom to look at herself. Her face was swollen so that her eyes were only slits. Red marks covered her back from her shoulders to her thighs. She drew a bath and carefully climbed into it and let her tears run freely down her face. Only when the water became uncomfortably cold did she finally lift her body out of the tub. She brushed her teeth, combed her hair and dressed in a loose-fitting jump suit.

Still wary, she quietly went downstairs and peeked into the guest room. He had not slept there either. The kitchen was like they had left it the day before. Lysa poured herself orange juice and pulled out a protein bar. She took her purse and keys and drove herself to the emergency room in the hospital. She needed to know that the life inside her was okay.

The nurse that admitted her asked about her condition. Lysa lied. "I was putting up drapes in our guest room and fell off the ladder, hitting a coffee table." The nurse was not convinced and when

Lysa was examined by the doctor he asked if she would like to lay charges against whomever had done this to her. Lysa repeated her lie. The doctor continued to examine her and after taking a sonogram and telling her the fetus was unharmed, he gave her a card saying, "If you change your mind about laying charges, please call this number. They will help you find a safe place and provide counselling." She took the card, thanked the doctor and left.

She could have left him that day. She could have driven home to her mother's house and let him come back to an empty place. But she didn't. Lysa drove home went into their bedroom, undressed and went to bed. She slept until early next day, showered, dressed and examined her face. The swelling had receded but the tissue around her eyes and mouth had taken on the purplish color of someone in a fight. She wondered how Adolph was. He had not called her, and she was reminded of the days after Henricke's death when he had built a silent wall between them.

Lysa spent the remainder of the week working on her new line of maternity clothes. She e-mailed Caroline the specs and phoned the manufacturers regarding the fabrics and number of pieces that she wished to produce. Caroline had been excited by the designs and would be featuring it on their blog over the next several weeks. Lysa told her that the first order would be delivered to the store in four weeks.

The week also gave Lysa's body time to heal and by the week-end most of the discoloration in her face and on her back had disappeared. She was unsure whether Adolph would be home for the week-end or not but had cleaned the house and shopped for food in the event he came.

It was Sunday when she heard his car drive up. She went to greet him at the door. His face was dark, marked with the anger she had witnessed a week ago. She held the door for him without a word and closed it behind him and walked towards the kitchen where she turned on the coffee maker and sat to wait. Adolph took his things upstairs and returned without a word. He took the coffee she had made and only then said to her, "I've made an appointment for us at the abortion clinic for Monday. I took the day off to drive you there and home again."

Lysa took a deep breath and said, "We need to talk about this Adolph. This is your baby."

"What do you take me for, Lysa," he hissed, "a complete fool? This thing is probably Bob's who's been sniffing around you like a tom cat sniffing a female in heat. We'll talk after you get rid of that thing." He stared at her icily and turned to go into his office.

"Vasectomies are not always perfect" Lysa called after him. Lysa then knew what she needed to do. She went upstairs to their room, pulled the suitcase out of the closet and filled it with the things she would need when she went back to her mother's place.

From behind the closed door, Adolph's voice sliced her heart like steel, "An abortion Lysa. That is final." Once finished, she snapped the suitcase shut, and rolled it out of the room. She had not heard Adolph come up the stairs. He stared at her with cold anger. "What do you think you're doing?"

"I'm going to my mother's, Adolph. I will not abort our child." She pushed past him to the stairs. Adolph grabbed at her hand that was pulling the suitcase. "No way are you going! And no way are you going to keep that thing."

She struggled to get away from him and felt his hand loosen hers as she fell backward down the stairs still clinging to the suitcase. She had heard the frightened yell "Lysa!" and then it was over.

Adolph was standing, holding her hand when she awoke. She looked around; two police, a doctor, two nurses with Adolph standing by the bed where she lay. She closed her eyes again. "What happened? Why am I here?"

She heard a voice, "Can we ask you some questions, Mrs. Stone?" Lysa tried to move her arm to support herself into a sitting position and winced as she became aware of the intravenous needle in her hand. "I can adjust the bed for you, Mrs. Stone". A different voice from just behind her spoke even as she felt the upper end of the bed lift her into a sitting position. She relaxed and opened her eyes again. "What happened? Why am I here?" Adolph, still holding her hand, answered in a flat voice, "You fell down the stairs, Lysa. You were dragging a suitcase and fell down the stairs."

"We need to ask you what happened, Mrs. Stone. Are you strong enough to answer some questions now?" It was the voice of the first person who had asked her that question a few moments earlier. She turned to the police officer and said, "Yes. I can answer whatever I can remember."

"Then I'll ask Mr. Stone to please leave until we are finished." And turning to Adolph she asked that he leave. Adolph held

Lysa's hand more tightly. "My wife needs me now. She just had a terrible accident. I am not going to leave her. Besides, I can fill in the things that she doesn't remember."

"Tell you what, Mr. Stone," the second officer said, "come with me. We'll have a coffee together and you can tell me what happened. That way we get the full story." His voice was firm so that the gentleness in the words did not betray his intent—Adolph was going whether he liked to or not.

As the two strode out together, the female officer pulled up a chair to the bed. "Start, wherever you like, Mrs. Stone. We have the statements from the ambulance attendants as well as the doctor who examined you and the nurses who have been with you the whole time."

Lysa looked at the officer first and then turned to the doctor. "My baby; what has happened to my baby?"

The doctor's voice was warm and soft. It reminded her of her dad's voice when he came to her room to quieten her after a nightmare. "I'm sorry, Mrs. Stone, but you lost the baby in the fall. You also have several broken ribs and a dislocated shoulder. Your ribs and shoulder will heal but your heart will take much longer. We can assist you with a counsellor before you leave the hospital but talking to the officer about everything that happened to bring you here today will be the start of that healing." He gave her arm a light squeeze and left along with the two nurses.

Lysa felt tears running down her face. "I'm not sure I can tell you much. Adolph and I had a fight about the baby. He wanted me to get an abortion. He thought that the baby wasn't his because he had a vasectomy years ago. But I know it was his. I never slept with anyone except my husband. He was my first and only sex partner."

The officer sat quietly taking notes. "Was the fight physical?" she asked. Lysa closed her eyes to picture what had gone on before the fall.

"Not really," she said. "Adolph told me he had made an appointment with an abortion clinic. I had said we needed to talk but he was unwilling to hear that it was his baby. I had told him earlier that he was welcome to take a paternity test, but once my husband makes up his mind it is difficult for him to change. He went to his office and I went upstairs to pack my suitcase. I was going to go back to my mother's until he saw sense." Lysa grimaced as she said, "saw sense". "And then what happened?" the officer asked.

I was rolling the suitcase out of the bedroom when I saw Adolph at the top of the stairs. He asked me what I was doing, and I told him I was leaving. He put his hand over mine and said that I was not going to leave. He held the hand that was pulling the suitcase. I struggled and kept pulling and I remember falling still holding onto the suitcase. I don't know if he let go or if I pulled free, but I was too close to the steps and lost my footing. I remember he yelled my name as I fell. He sounded scared. And then I woke up here."

The officer thanked Lysa and said, "Do you wish to lay charges against Mr. Stone?"

Lysa looked at her puzzled. "For what? For wanting me to have an abortion? For not believing that the baby was his?"

"No," she said, "for interfering with your leaving which resulted in the fall."

Lysa closed her eyes. It would be so easy to say "yes" but what would be gained? And so, she said, "No. This wasn't his fault. We both need to take responsibility for what happened."

"Take care Mrs. Stone. If you ever need to talk further about this or anything else in your life, give me a call." She handed Lysa a card and left.

Lysa felt empty. She closed her eyes to keep from crying, but the tears began to roll down her face again. Nothing hurt as much as the emptiness in her belly.

When Adolph returned and asked how things went, all she could do was shake her head and clench her teeth so that the scream inside her remained silent. Adolph told her that he had called her mother and she would be down as soon as the speed limit and line-up at the border would allow it.

"Thank you" she said and then the dam broke into uncontrolled sobbing. Adolph went for the nurse and then, giving Lysa a light kiss on the forehead, said he would leave so she could rest.

Lysa moaned. She longed for his arms to hold her; to tell her that he loved her; to tell her he was sorry that she lost the baby; to tell her that he believed her. But she was alone with the nurse and so she simply said that she wanted to sleep. The nurse rolled down the bed, gently covered Lysa with the blanket and turned down the lights in the room.

Her sleep was deep, and she woke with a start when she felt a hand caressing her face. Before even a sound came from her mouth, she saw the face of her mother hovering over hers, murmuring "My baby. My baby."

Lysa stretched out her arms as best as she could and welcomed her mom's embrace. Her tears mingled with the tears on her mother's face as the two women held one another.

After some time, they let go and Lysa's mother sat on the chair the officer had pulled up hours ago. "Can you tell me what happened, Lysa? Adolph said you fell down the stairs trying to get a suitcase down. What were you doing?"

Lysa re-told the story without the details that led up to the fall. She said she and Adolph had an argument about keeping the baby. He didn't want to be a father and they had never discussed having children. He wasn't ready and wanted her to have an abortion. She had told him she wasn't going to have one and was going home to stay with you until the baby was born. He didn't want her to go so she pulled at the suitcase and lost her footing on the top step. In the fall she had broken some ribs, dislocated her shoulder and lost the baby. At that point, Lysa again began to cry.

Her mom gently stroked her face allowing Lysa to sob until the tears dried up and then said, "You can come home with me and I'll look after you until you're healed."

"Thanks, mom." Lysa closed her eyes and let the fatigue of the day swallow her into sleep once again.

She woke next day to find a bouquet of flowers on her bedside table. The card said, "Thank you Lysa. Please come home," and was signed by Adolph.

"Thank you? Why 'thank you?' Why not 'I'm sorry.' Why not 'I love you'? Are you thanking me for not charging you? Are you thanking me that you don't have to shoulder the responsibility for the loss of our child? What is this insane 'thank you?'" She tore the card up but left the flowers sitting on the table. "Please come home," she mused, "Why should I? Why shouldn't I just go home with mom? Are you going to work on your angry outbursts? Are you going to believe me? Are you wanting our marriage to work? Give me some reasons Adolph that I should go home again."

Almost on cue, Adolph walked through the door and sat down beside her. He reached for her hand, but she pulled it away. "That was a terrible accident, Lysa. You don't know how much you scared me. I thought that I had lost you when I saw you crumpled at the bottom of the stairs, bleeding. All I could do was yell your name over and over, but you didn't respond. It took the ambulance forever to come and I just sat there beside you, watching the life flow out of you. Your mom said she will take you home to care for you but please come home to me. Your mom can come and stay and help take care of you, but I need you there Lysa. I need you at home."

He had given her the reason; he needed her at home. Lysa reached for his hand, gently squeezed it and said, "Thank you. I'll ask mom if she can stay a while with us. I'll come home."

She saw the relief in his eyes, like a little child who had been caught smoking behind the house, expecting a severe consequence and instead finding forgiveness by a loving parent. He kissed her forehead. "I'll be gone for three days at work, but I'll be back in time to take you home. I spoke with the doctor, he figures you should be okay to leave about that time."

She squeezed his hand, smiled, and told him she would be ready.

Lysa's mother stayed with them for four weeks before returning home. They worked in the garden, took long walks, visited with neighbours and talked. Her mom took on the job of cooking and cleaning when Lysa rested or worked on her designs. It was comforting for both women to spend the time together and especially heartening to Lysa that Adolph and her mom continued to build a strong relationship when he came home on the week-ends. When Lysa watched Adolph with her mom she felt so sure that things would work out between Adolph and herself, but when she was alone with him, in their bedroom, she saw the gulf that lay between them. "Could they ever get over what happened? Could she ever trust Adolph again? Would he ever learn to trust her?" They had not spoken about the loss of the baby or even about Lysa's fall on the stairs. They spoke about work, about the weather, about the garden and how pleasant it was to have Lysa's mom with them. They did not even speak about the reason that her mom was there.

But the healing was real. Lysa's mom talked about how well Lysa's ribs and arm were healing, how her color was coming back to normal, and how walking was strengthening the leg muscle that had been sprained in the fall. Over dinner one evening, she asked Adolph and Lysa if they would try for a child again soon. But when both looked at their plates, she said, "I'm sorry. It is too soon. You are both still raw from the accident that lost your child. Please forgive me." She reached out to touch Lysa's hand and saw the tears falling from Lysa's face into her plate. Adolph awkwardly put his arm around Lysa and said, "Come on. Lie down on the couch for a while and rest." And turning to her mom, he said, "She needs her mom. You go with her and I'll clean up." Hearing those words which she knew her mom heard as kindness while her ears heard his accusation, Lysa cried even more.

The last week-end that Lysa's mom was with them, Adolph invited Wendy and Gerry and Mike and Mary to a barbecue. And when the following day Lysa's mom gave her daughter a hug, she said, "You will be okay, Lysa. You have kind friends and a husband that is trying his best to help you. Don't work too hard and give yourself lots of opportunities to talk with your friends when Adolph is away."

Lysa smiled at her mom, keeping the tears under control, "I will mom. Be safe driving home and phone me when you get there." She paused, wrapped her arms around her mother and said, "I love you. Thanks for all you have done these four weeks. I don't think I could have handled it without you." She let go, watched her mom get into the car and stood waving until the car had left the driveway and had turned down the street.

Lysa stopped her thoughts at this point, looked at her empty tea-cup and wondered out loud, "Why didn't I just pack up and go home with mom? I knew that the black cloud that hovered over our bed when Adolph was home was antecedent to a storm that was kept only under control by the presence of mom. And why didn't I talk to mom about what was happening in our marriage; what really was the cause of Adolph's mood? I let mom think he was grieving the loss of the child and my battered body. I knew that something I said or did would trigger the violence again and yet I kept stumm."

She knew the answers to her rhetorical questions. She still held hope that they could work through their differences. She had rehearsed her defense so many times in her head that she was sure that she could convince her husband that the baby was his.

And she had not yet allowed her deepest fear, that Adolph had orchestrated her fall, rise to the surface of her mind to be examined by her in the cold, hard hours of her lonely state.

No. Going home would have signalled to her that her marriage was over; that Adolph's past had taken hold of her present and would not change. She was not yet ready to give up on him or their marriage.

"There are a lot of myths about love that is wrapped in flowers and pink tissue as if it were fragile and easily bruised but in reality love is hard as steel," she thought. She could no more bend her heart than one could have bent an iron bar.

She breathed in audibly. Inside her she felt the love she had felt for her husband rise out of the pain, beaten and bloodied but needing her to recognize it as love. Lysa allowed the tears she had held back now for so long to flow from her eyes; the tears that had stopped the night after her mother left them; the tears that he had beaten out of her after he had raped her.

She had nothing left after the night she lost the baby; no ideas on how to win him back; no energy to be anything except what he wanted at the moment. She became a stranger to herself and to her friends, a polished coffin exterior with living corpse inside. She buried herself in her work, entertained the neighbours at Adolph's behest, re-styled her wardrobe to cover the marks of his beatings, and no longer made the drive to Vancity to visit her mother or the store. She let the license on her car lapse too fearful to leave the house for any length of time lest Adolph come home and not find her there.

Adolph came home more often, surprising her with his arrival at odd hours in the day or night. She stopped being surprised so that her anxiety levels never ceased. Lysa knew her anxiety made things worse. She didn't know what to say when he asked questions about her work or where she had been or why she was in bed early or still awake late. She knew her timidity in answering him only made things worse. She knew that it was her own fault when he hit her because she couldn't really answer his questions properly. She knew she had become as pathetic as he said she was. She didn't want to be pathetic; she wanted to be his princess again and so when he had said she was dowdy, she really had wanted to take a good look and make herself the Lysa he had fallen in love with.

Lysa pulled a tea towel from the oven handle to mop her face. Letting her tears run freely had given her a sense of peace that she barely recognized and then she thought she heard, “My peace I give to you,” and holding the towel in front of her face she fell to her knees and cried out, “Lord, if you are real, help me tonight. Let me live.”

The same strength she had felt in the morning when she discovered her old self, filled her again as did a calm like that of a child who is holding fast to her father’s hand. She stood up just in time to see the lights of the car turned off and the motor shut down. She picked up a mug from the dishes assembled on the counter and waited for Adolph to come through the door.

“What do you think you’re doing?” he shouted as his eyes focused on Lysa.

She threw the mug so that it broke at his feet and with a calm, commanding voice, answered, “Don’t take another step this way.”

He laughed and started towards her. Lysa took another mug and threw it, and then the cup she had used for her tea.

"You're crazy", he yelled. "That was my grandmother's tea cup." He took another step towards her but more cautiously this time.

"It was my tea cup, Adolph. The one your grandmother gave me. Come any closer and I'll break all the dishes she gave us just as you broke me. So, step back and listen."

Lysa was surprised that Adolph did take a step back and let his hands hang slack by his sides. "You filthy trollop!" he hissed.

"I am not a prostitute. I am not a trollop or any of the other names you ascribe to me. I am your wife, Adolph. I loved you through the death of Henricke. I loved you through the death of our child."

He was about to take a step forward. She saw his jaw clenched and the hands by his side curl into a fist. She threw another cup at his feet. "Yes, your child, Adolph. I was the most loyal wife a man could have. I took your anger, your beatings, your words of derision and let them mold me into something that neither you or I recognized any longer. But today it's over. I am going back to Vancity and the only way that you can stop me is to kill me."

Adolph stared at her, his jaw now slackening. He took his car keys from his pocket and threw them at his feet among the chards of china. "Go then," he shouted, "I don't need you to tell me what you are. I know what you are." He turned away and went up the stairs to their room.

Lisa took the bag she had packed earlier along with her purse from the cupboard that had held the dishes, listened for sounds that might signal that her husband was waiting for her on the stairs. She heard the water in the shower being turned on, took a deep breath, walked across the room, picked up the keys and left the house. She threw the bag and purse on the passenger seat, started the engine and buckled herself in. She drove slowly down the driveway looking back to see if he had changed his mind. Only when she had turned the car onto the road did the peace she had felt leave her and she dissolved in fear. Sweat poured from every pore in her body; her hands shook so that she gripped the wheel more tightly. She put her foot on the gas and sped, guiding the car more by instinct than control until she reached the border. Not certain that his Nexus pass was still valid, she merged into a lane that seemed shorter than the others. Her heart was pounding so hard and her hand shook so severely that she almost dropped her passport trying to give it to the border guard.

"Are you okay, madam?" he inquired. "You are shaking."

Lysa felt her throat tighten. Her voice croaked, "I'll be okay. Thanks. I just need to get home."

"Where's home?" he asked, looking at Lysa intently.

"Vancity."

"So, what brings you back home to Vancity after such a lengthy stay here in the U.S.?" The voice was more insistent although still kindly.

Lysa chocked, "My husband. I mean I'm leaving my husband. Please, just let me go home."

"Do you need me to call someone to help you? Are you afraid that he's coming after you?" His hand held the passport out to her but not quite in reach.

Lysa looked at the man for the first time and saw the compassion in his eyes. She shook her head, "No, sir. I don't think he's following me tonight. I'll be okay now." She reached for the passport which he now extended into her hands. "Thank you," she said, "you are very kind."

The peace had returned. She closed the window and slowly drove in the direction home, turned into a Best Western hotel, and fell into bed. It was 11:30 next morning when the maid knocked on her door. "Will you be staying another day, madam? I can come back later to do up the room."

Lysa did not remember what she had told the desk clerk the night before but decided she needed the rest. "Yes, I'm staying another day. Thank you. I'll call housekeeping when I am ready to have the room made up." She heard the maid move the cart farther down the hall, opened a bottled water from the guest basket and drank before falling back into bed to sleep.

It was evening when she woke again. She showered, ordered a light dinner from the room service menu, poured herself a glass of wine from the mini bar, and turned on the television. She needed a mindless movie that she could watch while eating before she could begin to think about what she needed to do next.

By the time the movie had ended, Lysa had decided that she needed to get away—get away from everything, her work, her husband, even her mother. She made the decision to book a ten-day vacation in Spain and spent the next several hours surfing the net until she had found the perfect place—a one-bedroom Airbnb in Poiente Mayorka. She booked her flight to Portevera and a car rental. She e-mailed Carol to let her know that she would be on vacation and when everything had been completed, Lysa returned to bed and slept soundly until eight the next morning. She had breakfast in the hotel, packed her small bag and phoned her mother.

"I left Adolf. It's a long story, mom, and when I get back from Spain—yes, I really need a holiday to clear my mind—I'll tell you that story.

I've booked my flight for today and will be home in 10 days. I let Carol know I'll be away and am not saying where I'm going so that if Adolf asks you or her neither of you need to make up stories. You just don't know.

Please don't worry, I'm not going anywhere dangerous. No, no remote place either. It is quite civilized." Lysa laughed, said goodbye and hung up.

And then she laughed again, loudly. How long had it been since she laughed from the inside out like this? It felt as if a tight band around her chest had been cut so that she could breathe in deeply and expel her breath in the wonderful sound of laughter. She was still laughing when she went to the elevator, laughing as she paid her bill, and laughing as she stepped into the taxi that would take her to the airport. She was free.

The ten days alone in Spain gave Lysa the clarity that she had hoped for. She spent her time praying, walking along the beach for hours, relaxing on the patio with a cool drink in the afternoon and going to dinner in the evening. She hadn't brought anything with her outside what she had taken from the house in Bellaire, but she needed little. She purchased a bathing suit, a beach cover-up, shorts and a couple of tops, a three-piece outfit that she wore to dinner and a pair of sandals. She chose to frequent a small Spanish restaurant within walking distance of the condo and sat under the vines that covered a tiled courtyard at a table for one. She ordered the daily special—most often a combination of fish and rice—a glass of wine and quietly ate her meal as she read from the small Gideon Bible that she had taken from the night-stand at the Best Western Hotel. When the light no longer allowed her to read, she would walk back to her condo, shower, pull on her nightshirt, turn the radio to a classical music station and sit by the window meditating on the passages she had read earlier until sleep overtook her.

By the time she flew back to Vancity she knew what she needed to do beginning with an honest discussion of her life with Adolf with her mom. It had not been easy to tell her mom the events that had lead up to her leaving Adolf. Part of her still wanted to protect Adolf and their relationship and part of her knew that her mom deserved to know the truth. She had prayed that the Lord would give her the words that her mom could hear without making him sound like a monster. Yes, the things that he had done to her were monstrous, but she had examined her life in the hours before he had returned, the hours that she had believed would be her last, and she had seen the opportunities that she had wasted that could have changed her life long before that hour. The outcome would have been the same—she would have left, but the pain and damage to herself could have been averted. It was not fault-finding. She knew it wasn't her fault, but rather an abdication of herself. "I have learned mom," she spoke quietly, firmly, "to not ignore the voice inside of me. God, through your and dad's teachings, through Henricke's frankness, let me know who Adolf was. He was not a monster, he fell back into the monstrous beliefs he had learned as a child and youth. I have no doubt he loved me—at least initially, before jealousy and possessiveness began to eat him up. The only example he had for dealing with a woman was to not trust her and to punish her for every transgression he believed about her. My part in all this was to love him as I believed I wanted him to be and therefore constantly making excuses for him—first to others and finally to myself. I began to believe that I was the problem; that if I were different, if I were able to see how tired he was or stressed or upset he was by his work or my work that he would be the kind and attentive man I had fallen in love with. I made the same mistake Adolf did—believing that another person could fill the hole we all have inside us, the hole that only God can fill."

Lysa's mom had interjected several times during the story and said that she wondered, when Lysa had called to say she was going on a vacation without saying where that there was more to this break-up than her daughter had said. She told Lysa that Adolf had contacted her the week she was in Puento Mayorga but after learning that she didn't know where Lysa had gone, he had not contacted her again.

When Lysa had finished, her mom put her arms around her daughter, her eyes wet with tears, and said, "My dear, dear daughter. I'm so sorry that you couldn't tell me sooner. I could tell things weren't what they should be when I came to look after you after you lost the baby, but I didn't want to pry. And you kept reassuring me that things were okay. Please forgive me Lysa. I am so sorry."

Lysa held her mom. "No need to apologize. I kept you at arm's length because I was still under the illusion I could fix this; I could fix Adolf." Lysa grinned at her mom. "Superwoman just had to learn on her own that no one except God can fix a person—and then only if they want to be fixed."

Lysa moved back into her mother's house. She converted the den into her design room and purchased new equipment. The thought of going back to Bellaire to get her things was still something she avoided. She was glad that Adolf seemed to have accepted her leaving and did not try to contact her.

Lysa confided her story to Carol who offered to sell back her share of the business now that Lysa was back but Lysa declined. "We have a great partnership, Carol. You have done an amazing job with the web-site and the store. Why would I ever want to dissolve the partnership?" They both laughed and hugged one another.

"Well then, partner," Carol said as she let go of Lysa, "I think we need to hire another full-time sales person. Amy really likes dealing with the on-line orders and has done a wonderful job, but I think that if we continue to expand in that area—and we will if our service continues to be great—Amy will have more than enough to do in that area. We need another person who is equally committed to our store as Amy is."

Work kept Lysa busy. They hired a business graduate from Kwantlen College as the new sales person. Victoria was not only personable, she had a genuine gift for displaying merchandise and soon the store had an updated look of a fine boutique—fashions complete with accessories such as unique pieces of costume jewelry and one of a kind handbags that were made in Vancity.

Nevertheless, Lysa felt an increasing unease as the days rolled into weeks without a word from Adolf.

“I don’t even know what I would say to him,” she said to her mom a month after she had returned from Spain. “But the longer we don’t talk, the more antsy I’m getting.”

“Maybe he knows that about you Lysa; knows that you would begin to worry and that gives him back some of the power that he lost when you walked out.”

Lysa mulled her mom’s words over in her mind. “You could be right, mom. I think I will need some help with this.”

She phoned her pastor when they had finished dinner, apologizing for calling him at home and laid out her situation. She had met with Pastor Kuehn after returning from Spain and had told him about her marriage and her new born faith. He had connected her with a Bible study group made up of people that varied in age from late teen to eighty-three years. It was a lively group and she enjoyed their discussions and the increasing friendships that were forming.

Pastor Kuehn gave Lysa the name of a counsellor who had recently retired from her job but who had told the pastor that she would be happy to speak to people going through difficult times as long as he kept the numbers low enough, so she wouldn’t feel as if she were still working. Lysa thanked him for his help, wrote the name and phone number on a small card and put it into her purse.

She called the number Pastor Kuehn had given her the next morning. "Hello Patti. My name is Lysa. Pastor Kuehn gave me your name and phone number and said you might have some time to see me." Lysa quickly outlined her background and current situation and was gratefully surprised to hear that Patti could see her the following day. They would meet at the coffee shop near her store and get to know one another over a coffee before making a commitment to meet over Lysa's problem. Lysa felt elated.

Patti was a warm, open, lady whose eyes shone as she talked about her own journey to faith and her profession. She had been a family counsellor and over the years had met with couples in abusive relationships. "It's not always the men," she quipped, "some women can be very abusive. Women tend more towards emotional abuse while men more often are physical abusers. But from what you told me, it seems your husband began as an emotional abuser and escalated to physical abuse. But we'll talk more about that if you feel comfortable enough with me to continue as a client."

Lysa was more than comfortable. She felt that she had been heard more deeply than she had even expressed herself and agreed to meet once a week in Patti's office at her home. Patti said that she charged a sliding fee. Those who could pay the full amount would; those who could only pay a portion, would; and those who could not afford to pay anything could get her services free of charge. "The people who pay the full amount cover the cost of those who cannot pay at all. Anything I have left over after my expenses are covered I give to our mission's outreach at the church." Lysa said she could afford the full amount and would be glad to do so. They shook hands and Lysa returned to the store.

"I've arranged for some counselling for me" she said to Carol later in the day.

"Good for you girl. You flinch every time a man looks like he's coming into the store. That's no way to live. You got to get this monkey off your back—if you pardon the cliché," she laughed.

Lysa laughed as well.

"It's good to hear you laugh again," said Carol when they had both stopped laughing, "you had become so serious it was disconcerting at times."

"No promises," grinned Lysa, "but I will begin to hone my mirthfulness a little more regularly."

The two friends looked at each other warmly and returned to their work.

The weeks rolled into months. Lysa met with Patti each week and slowly the edges of fear began to disappear, and the inner joy began to again take root. Christmas passed without word from Adolf although with Patti's encouragement Lysa had sent a card to him.

"One of you needs to break this silence, Lysa," she had said. "Eventually you and he will need to deal with the next step in your relationship. Either you get a divorce, or you work toward reconciliation. But both options need to be talked about. You don't need to write anything if you don't want to, just get a card with the usual 'Merry Christmas; Happy New Year' and sign your name. It's a start."

Nevertheless, when a small bouquet of yellow tea roses along with a brown envelope was delivered by a courier, Lysa's gut knotted and she had to sit down to sign for the delivery. She tossed the flowers into the garbage and was about to shred the letter without opening it when she realized that the return address on the envelope was from a law firm in Bellaire. She put the letter into her purse and did not take it out again until she was at home. Pouring herself a glass of wine first, she sat at the kitchen table and slowly opened the letter. It was a form filing for divorce.

She found herself becoming angry. “How dare you!” she shouted. Her mom came into the kitchen to see whom her daughter was shouting at. Lysa pointed at the letter, and shouted, “He wants a divorce. He was the one abusing me, and he is asking for a divorce. And he sends it along with yellow roses. The insufferable snake!” She threw the letter to the floor and slammed her hand on the table before dissolving in tears.

Lysa’s mom put her arms around her daughter and let her cry. When the sobbing abated, her mom pulled up a chair beside Lysa and still keeping one arm around her daughter asked quietly: “He’s opened up a lot of wounds again. I’m so sorry Lysa, but this time you won’t have to walk through it alone. I’m here for you and whatever you decide, I’ll support you in that.”

Lysa snuggled into her mother’s embrace and for a while the two women sat together in silence. At last Lysa whispered hoarsely,

"I want a divorce. It's just that I thought I should be the one who initiated that. I wanted to do that in person. I wanted to tell him how much he hurt me; how much I had loved him and how much I had wanted our marriage to work. I wanted him to know what he did to us, to our baby, to our hopes and dreams. I wanted him to suffer as I suffered. I just wasn't ready to meet him yet. Maybe this is best. Maybe never seeing him is the best thing for me. Maybe he is suffering and that is why he sent the roses along with the divorce papers. Maybe he thought he could change things." Lysa sat up straight and looked at her mom and raised her voice in affirmation, "Well it's not going to happen. Yellow roses are no longer an apology. He will get these papers faster than he could ever have imagined. I'm signing tonight and will have them couriered to him tomorrow." She picked up her glass, held it up as if to give a toast and said, "Here's to a new life." She tipped the glass up and drained it.

Lysa delivered the envelope containing her divorce paper to the courier herself. She had not entered into a contest with Adolph about ownership of anything that they had in common. She simply wanted to end the marriage. But she was glad that she could see Patti later that day and unburden herself from the emotions that the papers had raised. While Carol thought she should have taken the papers to a lawyer before signing anything, Patti did not question her decision. For Lysa signing the papers had been cathartic and the first step towards her independence. Patti would help her to begin to walk this new road.

Six weeks later, Lysa received word that the divorce was registered in the provincial legislature as well as Washington. She was free. It came therefore as a surprise when a letter from Adolph arrived at her mother's home a week later.

Dear Lysa,

I am selling the house in Bellaire as well as Henricke's house in Vancity after I return from a three-week sales trip the middle of next month. I am hoping that you still have the keys to the Bellaire house so that you can take the opportunity of my absence to pick up your things and any items that you would like to keep from our time together. If you do not have a key, I have left instructions and a spare key with my lawyer. As my work has brought me farther south, I have decided to re-locate to Arizona.

Sincerely yours,

Adolph

Again, Lysa felt the anger rise up in her throat. Maybe she should have taken Carol's advice and seen a lawyer. He's going to sell the houses. He's going to relocate to Arizona. He's going to feather his nest and she can pick out what she might want from their "time together". She spat out the two words. But she would go and get her stuff. She wouldn't take one thing from that house that wasn't hers. He could do whatever he wanted with the rest.

Lysa picked up the phone and called Bob and Elizabeth. Elizabeth answered the phone. "Hi Elizabeth. It's me Lysa."

"Lysa! How wonderful to hear your voice again. How are things going? What are you up to? I see you have increased the staff at your shop. I love the designs on the web-site..." Elizabeth rattled off the questions and statements as if shot from an automatic rifle.

Lysa laughed. "Woah, Elizabeth. One question at a time. I'm not doing too badly and yes; the store is doing really well. What I'm phoning you for is to see if that rain-check for a stay at your place could still be cashed in; that is if I'm not being too presumptuous."

"That would be awesome" Elizabeth chirped. "When can you come?"

"I'd love to come at the end of the month if that is okay. But I may as well be honest with you before you commit to my stay. I haven't been over the border since I left almost eighteen months ago. I haven't even been able to call and chat with you or the others even though I know I owe you a huge explanation. But I have been getting counselling and that has helped. Adolph is putting the house up for sale next month and he asked if I could clear out my things before that."

"The nerve…" Elizabeth interjected.

"Yah. That was my first reaction only a little more vehemently." Lysa laughed. "Anyway, I'll sit and tell you the whole story when I come—that is if I may come."

"Of course, you can come. I count you among one of my dear friends and I am so glad that you are finally able to come and see us. You may want to know that we have all been praying for you, so this is the answer to our prayers. Can you stay a week or even longer?"

"I hadn't really thought about how long to stay but yes, I can stay a week. Thank you; thank you; thank you. I'll drive down the last

Saturday of the month after work, so I should be at your place around eight, and I'll stay until the following Friday."

They bid each other good-bye and Lysa hung up the phone. She felt a lot lighter. "Thank you for my friends, Lord," she breathed, "I never knew that they were believers. I guess it wasn't just coincidence that you put this hedge around me when I married Adolph."

"They prayed for me," she continued to muse, "I still have so much to learn about Christians." Somewhere out of nowhere she heard "Yes you do girl" and suddenly she found herself laughing until the tears ran down her eyes.

"Was that you God or was it just me talking to myself?" she asked out loud. There was no answer this time. She would need to take this to her pastor. Does God really talk?

The two weeks before Lysa left for Bellaire flew by quickly. The changes from summer to fall and winter were always busy times in the store and even with the addition of Victoria months before, Lysa found that she spent most of her time with customers. It was great in some ways, but it also ate into her time to design and create proto-types for the following year and with a week looming away from her office she suggested to Carol that they explore the possibility of hiring a sales person who would be on call, perhaps a college student with flexible hours. They spoke to Victoria who almost immediately lined up three students for them to interview. In the end two of the students, James and Jennifer, said they would be able to take on the job. Their hours were such that if one couldn't make it the other could. Carol, who would book their hours was tickled that both students' name started with "J". "All I need to do is book "JJ" and they can figure out who will come," she laughed after the interview.

Carol booked JJ in for three days the week that Lysa would be in Bellaire to allow for Victoria's and her own days off and to give the students a chance to see how their schedules would work out as well as how they would do in the retail business.

Lysa had packed her bag for the week in Bellaire Friday after work and threw it in the trunk of the car Saturday morning. She packed a sandwich, apple and a bottle of water to eat on her way. There was usually at least an hour's wait at the border—plenty of time to have dinner. She picked up a coffee on-route and found that the slow pace to the border control allowed her to eat in comfort. The moment Lysa had crossed the border she began to feel anxiety tug at the back of her throat. By the time she had passed the exit to Bliss the fear inside her exploded so that her hands shook so vehemently she knew she had to pull off the highway. Lysa shut off the motor and tried to pray. She found herself bathed in sweat, her throat almost closing her airways so that she was hyperventilating. She furiously called out to God to be released from the anxiety. Once again, she seemed to hear a calming voice in her head, "You don't need to do this alone, girl. Give Elizabeth a call."

Lysa stopped talking and listened intently to see if she could hear the voice again. She heard only her own breath which had now quietened. The restriction in her throat had also left her as had the sweat. She picked up her cell phone and called Elizabeth.

"I need your help. Don't think I'm losing it, Elizabeth but I just heard a voice that told me to call you because I don't need to do this alone. Please pray for me. I had a terrible anxiety attack just now crossing the border. Part of me is terrified that I will just turn around and go home."

"Oh, Lysa," she heard the warm, comforting voice of Elizabeth, "of course I will pray for you. Bob and I both will pray. Just trust the Lord that he will safely see you to our house, and we will trust Him to bring you safely here."

Lysa felt a weight being lifted from her chest. "Thank you, Elizabeth. I will see you in under an hour."

They said good-bye and Lysa merged back into the traffic and arrived at the house in forty minutes without further discomfort.

Bob and Elizabeth greeted Lysa at the door and hugged her warmly. "Welcome, welcome! It is so good to see you again," they both said in almost unison.

"We've got your room all set for you, Lysa," said Elizabeth, as Bob took her small suitcase from her hand and lead her through the living room to the back of the house where the guest room was located.

"Take your time to freshen up," said Bob, as he placed the suitcase on a chair beside the bed, "we have a chardonnay chilling and Elizabeth has put together some small bites for us when you are ready."

Lysa thanked him as he closed the door on his way out and sat on the side of the bed looking out onto the garden that was quickly becoming dark with the encroaching evening. She suddenly felt overwhelmingly tired and would have easily dropped off to sleep except that she knew her hosts were waiting for her in the living room. Lysa went to the washroom and splashed water on her face. It felt good. She opened her suitcase and pulled out her slippers that she put on. She slipped out of her business clothes and into a colorful Mumu that she had packed instead of a housecoat. She felt dressed but comfortable and went to meet her hosts.

A cool glass of wine and a small plate of dried fruits, nuts and cut cheeses greeter her as they sat down to chat. Bob and Elizabeth talked about what had happened in their life the past two years, how the neighbours had developed close friendships since the first barbecue at her house, and the joy of being "grandparents" to Wendy and Gerry's twins. They brought out pictures of the twins who were now active toddlers getting into all kinds of mischief. They saw the tiredness on Lysa's face and graciously called it a day. They did not ask Lysa about her story and she was grateful to them for filling the evening with their own stories.

Lysa woke up early Sunday morning. She showered and dressed for church. The house was still very quiet but when she tiptoed to the kitchen she found Elizabeth and Bob already there making coffee and heating a griddle for pancakes and bacon. Lysa asked if they were going to church and when they said "yes", she asked if she could accompany them.

Unlike the small, quiet church she attended at home, Lysa was taken aback by the noisy chatter of perhaps 150 people of all ages greeting one another, laughing and bringing one another up-to-date on the week's happenings. Instead of the peaceful strains of a piano and violin in the sanctuary, she was greeted by guitars accompanied by a keyboard and drums. She had wanted to hide her fears about tomorrow in quietness and for a moment she wanted to turn back and leave the building, but Elizabeth and Bob guided her between handshakes with people they passed to seats in the center of the church. People around them were already standing, some raising hands, others clapping or tapping their feet to the music that seemed to fill the building. She was washed in an air of celebration. She felt new, reborn, and without thinking found her arms lifted and her voice raised with those around her in the worship of God. The prayers and the sermon all seemed to be directed at her, lifting the weight of tomorrow's visit to her and Adolph's home from her shoulders. It was as if God himself was speaking to her, reassuring her that all would be well and for the first time, as the congregation once again raised its voices in praise at the end of the service, Lysa understood what Paul meant when he wrote to the Thessalonians that they should give thanks to God in all circumstances.

"Yes," Lysa thought, "this service was crafted for me. It took my eyes off me and tomorrow and directed them to Jesus who is clearing the path for me. 'Thank you, Lord,'" she whispered.

On the way back, Lysa could not contain herself any longer. She thanked Bob and Elizabeth for taking her to church, told them what happened during the service and then poured out her story of fear of returning to the house that she had shared with her husband, her fear of re-living the emotions of love and pain and betrayal, and the cleansing of that fear as she worshipped God. She was still pouring out her story when they arrived back at Bob and Elizabeth's house so that Bob shut off the engine and they sat in the car until Lysa had finished. They were silent for a moment and then, in a clear soprano voice, Elizabeth began to sing "Amazing Grace" while tears ran down all of their faces and Bob kept quietly repeating "Thank you God. Thank you, Jesus. Thank you, thank you, thank you."

How long they sat and worshipped together Lysa would not remember. She only remembered the love that was in that car that day. And when Elizabeth offered to go with her the following day to help with the move, Lysa was able to say, "Thank you, Elizabeth, but I need to do this with only Jesus by my side. He has given me new life," she reached out and squeezed Elizabeth's shoulder, "and new friends—no better than that, a new family in Christ. I am learning that with Him all things are truly possible including moving out my things from a house that was filled with so much love and so much pain. Besides," she laughed, "I'll be coming back each evening to a fabulous meal with my new family that has shown me so much love."

Printed in the United States
By Bookmasters